ISBN 978-88-8398-070-1

Copyright ©2011 by European Press Academic Publishing
Firenze, Italy

www.e-p-a-p.com
www.europeanpress.eu
Proprietà letteraria riservata
Printed in Italy, USA and UK

Alison Castelli

Cauliflower Head

EUROPEAN PRESS ACADEMIC PUBLISHING
Fiction *Mariposa*

Prologue

NEW YORK CITY

My Walkman makes me feel free. When I trot down Broadway listening to Suzanne Vega's "Small Blue Thing," I am protected from men who call me names or ask me out. I can't hear them. I can't make out what the hell they are saying.

Whoever dreamt up the notion that "sticks and stones may break my bones, but names can never hurt me" must not have been a woman because, as I see it, I am rendered helpless by names. Last Sunday some punk called me "cauliflower head" while I was playing rugby in Central Park. Was it really true that my pinned-back, naturally curly hair—you know, in that middle phase between long and short—made me look as if I had a cauliflower for a head? After that I couldn't make a play in the scrum and I got so distracted that I let Betsy steal the ball right out of my hands. She put a dent in my left forearm to boot.

Maybe I am just particularly sensitive this year. The Democrats are becoming Republicans, the earth is warming up, and my sneakers are hurting my feet.

I flip off the Walkman and make my way to the seventh floor of the music building. Margaret, the overworked, bored administrator who dresses daily in a black smock, scowls at me, and I, in turn, wave to some lowly first-year student. In my mailbox is the fourth chapter of my dissertation, covered in red ink by Professor Vincent "Sparky" Sheppard—his middle name a result of years of coma-inducing graduate seminars. He has nothing particularly positive to say about my work, just the usual remarks about commas and typographical oversights. What about my ideas? Weren't they different? Wasn't I smart? Can't he tell?

I feel an avalanche of panic reassuring me that I am going nowhere fast in academia. I'm a failure—so familiar. What else is there to think? My lovers tell me that, as do my parents, my brother, and my starving artistic voice.

Hold on!

Things would be different this time. I'll correct the mistakes and move on. Gathering the remains of my ego, I turn on Suzanne Vega and walk proudly by the department office. The sun still shines on the sidewalk, baking the studded gum-droppings.

Things would be OK. . . .

I could not have done this a year ago. Let me tell you.

I was madly in love. Her name was Robin. She was thirty-two, an architect who worked for big Wall Street bank, and completely fucked-up. Of course, not quite as screwed-up as I was for dating her. She had a boyfriend in Pittsburgh whom had she dated for six years, demonic parents, no self-esteem, and a huge ego. A lethal combination. She had never "slept with a woman before" (oh my God) but had cheated many times on this boyfriend with pushy guys from work. She was incredibly sexy, with green eyes and brown wavy sassy hair, long sinuous legs, soft, full breasts, and an attitudinal problem. Perfect.

I met her on a rugby pitch on Long Island. We both played for this Irish coach over the summer. I watched her stretch. Her hand glided gently over her calves as her breasts protruded above the lip of her tank top. Her long neck reached toward her toes. It was warm and wet that summer day in Bethpage, and Tim had just yelled at me to quit dropping the ball and make a good tackle for once in my life. After hearing his words I sprinted to the woman carrying the ball and felt my right knee give way. Pain exploded in the joint. Robin came over to see if I was OK. In my feminine macho way I said, "no problem," hoping that she would never let me go. The rain that had collected on the front part of my head finally gushed down my face. I was done for the day.

Sports injuries have a certain bittersweet charm for any lesbian. While writhing in pain, we are surrounded by women who ask us whether we need anything and give us great big hugs. No pain, no gain.

We lost 11–3, and Tim called us a bunch of lazy, popcorn-eating Americans. Then he suggested we get a beer at the rural Bethpage bar down the street. Big American cars dotted the parking lot. Men with long beards and red faces walked in.

"Robin, could you get me a Coors Light on tap if possible?" I asked with my leg propped up on a chair. She walked across the room, sat down at the bar, and chatted with the big, hairy guy. No lesbian worth her salt would give guys at a bar a second look. Drunken men are more likely to call you a dyke. Shit, she is straight!

My knee throbbed, and Tim put a bag of ice on it. He was from Dublin and had come to the United States after his father told him that he was not good enough to play in the Irish Rugby League. He coached at a local junior high for a year, quit, and got into the cellular phone business. We never really knew exactly what he did for a living, except that he drove a Lexus through the streets of New York and slept with Wynette, the captain of our team. He was tall with beautiful green eyes, which, I'm pretty sure, he highlighted with some black eyeliner.

I liked him for the most part because he reminded me of my Italian mother. He yelled a lot, said that we "played a like a bunch of old ladies," and if it was late at night, drove each of us home so we wouldn't get mugged—or worse. This kind of messy juxtaposition of positive and negative feelings forms the basis of my neuroses. You'll see.

Robin handed me the tall, cold beer and sat down. Like an actor in a Chinese opera troop, her body moved in circles rather than in sharp angles. Her hands felt the air, and her thick lips gently parted as she spoke. Her bare leg brushed against mine. I experienced immediate sexual arousal.

No one knew about the momentous, all-encompassing "bombs away" transformation taking place inside of me. My metabolism was changing from "regular" to "out-of-control hyper-love." The gray sky outside portended joy, not sorrow. Tim was no longer a son of a gun, but a lost soul. My family was not a roadblock to healthy life, but a source of compassion and hope.

Love changed all—those chemicals, I mean.

Back on earth, Tim picked up the check at the bar and the team split up to return to various destinations in the New York area. I lived near Columbia University, so I drove the West Siders home. Debbie lived on East 85th Street and drove with Robin. Figures.

Chapter 1

I called Martha when I got home because I was feeling a little guilty. We had been seeing each other for three years before she decided to abandon me and go to Harvard Business School. This was her first semester.

"The school has its own gym and indoor tennis courts," she bragged. "But the people are sooooo superficial. Like, the women get dolled up to go to class, and the men wear jackets and ties." She paused. "I don't know how I'm going to fit in."

Despite being blond, blue-eyed, and six feet tall, she was the antithesis of conventional American beauty. She was beautiful all right, but in a more "competitive swimmer" way. With broad shoulders, deeply defined legs, and whiskers on her chin, she exuded confidence when she walked into a room.

She is probably one of the most extraordinarily gifted people I know: a great athlete, a brilliant student, a capable piano player. I met her playing basketball at Vassar College. She was my first WASP girlfriend with money. And though I do maintain a few crumbs of political correctness concerning the need for women to define themselves through more than their mate's money, dating Martha came as a welcome relief from the pressure of empty pockets. We could go to the movies every night if we wanted to and drink imported beers afterward. She always had money and was not weary of spending it—even a little on me.

Martha was gay through and through, and I felt both comforted by, and fearful of, that fact. She had a healthy dislike of most men for being men, and she refused to interact with people whom she deemed sexist, racist, or homophobic. She was completely out to her family. I was invited over to her family's Connecticut mansion for every major Christian holiday. Her mother was a violinist and her sister played the lute. They filled the enormously beautiful home with music.

I knew that Martha came from a real American family because her grandparents did not speak with an accent. Growing up in New York, I had never before met grandparents who did not have at least a slight—or, in the case of my Russian side of the family, heavy—accent, generally from an eastern European country. My grandmother still wrote "one hundred dallars" on my birthday check.

Martha and I stopped making love about a year and a half before she left for Boston. A clear instance of "lesbian death-bed," or "bed-death" (I can never get this straight), I just couldn't get myself to be intimate with her any more. She sweetly began by trying to kiss me, gently massaging my shoulders. I panicked.

"I'm sorry Martha. I'm too sleepy. Don't you have to get up early tomorrow for your meeting?"

This went on for nearly eight months until Martha finally gave up seducing me. I was totally and utterly relieved. I brainwashed myself into thinking that I did not have to have sex to be in a satisfying relationship. Martha and I had a great nonsexual, meaningful partnership.

I would not and could not talk about the problems with her. Why didn't she leave me? (Oh, right, she did.)

Days, weeks, and months passed. She supported me during those anxious times in graduate school: my master's exam, my first day of teaching, and my master's thesis. I helped her get through her job at the insurance company in midtown. We went on wonderful trips together to Spain, England, and Greece. Martha loved me and took care of me. She pumped the gas, paid the hotel manager, and asked for directions. I couldn't leave the safe confines of the car or hotel room because I was scared to get harassed for being gay by foreigners. As if anyone could tell.

Before moving to Boston, Martha lived in the Park Slope section of Brooklyn, fondly referred to as "Dyke Slope" by many in the neighborhood. First settled by Barnard College graduates in the late seventies, the neighborhood consisted of small brownstones arranged neatly in rows. Saturday nights were spent at women's dances at the community center, and Sundays playing softball in Prospect Park. Businesses were "gay-friendly" and harassment was not common.

Hello? Reality? Martha was getting tired of New York City and me. Both were devoid of honesty. New York gives you the impression that you are living life to the fullest, when, in reality, your body and mind are completely overrun by distractions, annoyances, and fears. Getting to work involves squeezing onto the train; some guy once masturbated against Martha's hand while she held on to the metal pole. (He came all over her new suit.) New Yorkers believe that this is a complete, fulfilling life experience, while living comfortably in a small town, tending to the garden, and teaching at the local school is pure hell.

Our relationship evolved under veils of dishonesty. The pressures of daily life in the city had created the illusion that things were moving to a higher realm of intimacy when things were stagnating. Dead.

"Maybe we should see a relationship counselor?" Martha asked me one Saturday morning in bed.

"No, sweetie," I responded quickly, without giving it any thought. "We just need to talk about it. How about later? Aren't you hungry? It's time for breakfast."

My natural impulse was to bail out of the relationship and

begin afresh with somebody else. Or was it to begin a new relationship then bail out of the present one? I had done one of the two options eight times previously. Martha shrugged her shoulders and rolled over on her side. She had to get out of this, but how?

The answer came June 15, the day Martha received news that Harvard Business School had accepted her for the fall semester. I was happy for her. We both knew that this was the only way to escape two dead-end positions: her job as an administrator at Equity Insurance and her job as mother and friend to me. She accepted the offer to attend without blinking an eye. We never even discussed the consequences to our relationship.

Fear enveloped my heart. I began to methodically set myself up for an emotional demolition. I had screwed up another good thing. Case closed.

Adding to the dreariness of my situation, I listened to the first message on my machine, which sounded something like, "Jean, dis is yur Mamma. Remember me? Plesa calla me samatime."

As if I didn't know who belonged to that accent. This was my mother's philosophy of child rearing at work, the "You'll appreciate me when I'm dead" school of mind control. Comprising a complex system of positive and negative stimuli, such as I love you, I hate you, you are great, you stink, the method has at its foundation one principle emotion: guilt. You should appreciate the endless—my endless—devotion to you children. If you don't, you are selfish ingrates, who use your mother as your slave for laundry and food.

In the hands of the seasoned Italian practitioner, guilt could get the kids to do just about anything—and my mother was a pro. Guilt could get the kids to clean their rooms, keep them quiet at the table, stop them from going out with friends, and perhaps most importantly for my mother, keep them forever devoted to Mamma. The method works like this: everything the kids did was a reflection of how much they cared about their Mamma. For example, when I had my heart set on joining the basketball team in high school, which my mother vehemently objected to because it was a boyish thing to do, she said that if I really loved her, I would choose to stay home in the afternoons to practice the piano because the sound of music in the house was the only thing that really ever made her happy. How could I take away the little joy she experienced in her life? I was self-serving and inconsiderate for even thinking of it. I never did join that basketball team. Afternoons were spent practicing the piano for some recital I didn't want to be in, in an itchy skirt and pinchy shoes. Evenings I shot hoops in the backyard, under the kitchen light that shined on the court.

Here is a test to see if you can master the "You'll appreciate me when I'm dead" method of mind control. A parent's nightmare: my brother wants to go out with his friends to see a rock concert in Manhattan on a Saturday night. How does a Mamma stop him from going?

a) Tell him it is too dangerous, and ask him not to go for her sake.

b) Tell him to talk to his father.

c) Call the police.

d) Say that if he does go, she'll be so worried that she won't be able to sleep, and she will suffer a stroke or heart attack during the night.

I think you get the point. If Fred goes, he runs the risk of causing a fatal injury to mother. If he doesn't, he loses out on an important adolescent experience and may be ridiculed by his friends. Anyway, stoned, Fred went to the concert. Mamma stayed up all night nagging me about how Fred was killed by a hostile mob, or how he ingested a drug laced with arsenic, or how he died in an automobile accident. She waited up all night swearing that he was dead. To this day, I cannot sleep when my lover stays out late for work. I imagine tragedy.

At least Fred went to the concert. I never did. I was the good girl who did not take chances that might disappoint Mamma. I stayed at home a lot and took care of my mother, whose husband was never around. In some bizarre sense, I was wife, husband, and daughter to Mamma.

She insulted me all the while. My hair was too bushy—so she cut it. My shirt was too sloppy—so she threw it out. My school essay was poorly written—so she told Dad to rewrite it.

Mamma was born in Cogne, a small town surrounded by white-peaked mountains that descend from Mont Blanc. The family once lived in a sprawling medieval house believed to have been the birthplace of Saint Anselm. A small alcove situated between the bathroom and verandah still holds a plaque commemorating the blessed event. Some years back my grandfather wrote a book arguing that Saint Anselm was not born in their house, but in Chatillon, another town down the valley. No one listened to him, and every summer eager medievalists came knocking on the door to see the home. He told them to get lost, with a gun in his hand.

There was no love lost between Nonno and the Catholics. He was excommunicated in 1925 for refusing to donate some of his land to the church so that they could enlarge the cemetery. As a result, he did not allow his devout Austrian-born wife to attend Mass and decided to give his three children non-Christian names. My mother is called Demetra; her brothers are Davide and Saul. Can you image growing up with the name Demetra in a small, conservative town where everybody is named Maria or Anna or a variation of both?

Nonno's family owned huge plots of land in the Alps: entire

mountains, fifty or so chalets, twenty apricot trees, and ten peach orchards. Most of the family's time was spent tending to these properties, and Mamma told me stories of Nonna washing the many flights of wooden stairs until he declared them clean. Mamma sewed draperies for the hundreds of windows, while the boys tended to leaky roofs and faulty plumbing. No one complained. Chores were completed. My mother has an excellent eye for home decorating.

Nonno was somewhat of a maverick for his time. He traveled to Boston in 1923 to learn English, and a few years later returned to Turin, where he taught English in the local high school. Meanwhile, he earned a law degree and tried some minor cases in court. After ten years of a grueling schedule, he retired and spent the rest of his life tending his homes and selling and buying coins. In his spare time, he feuded with all the other families about some political issue or another. He drove a fancy old Fiat with thick gray doors and was happy to learn that my mother was going to marry a Jew, since that meant Dad would certainly make a lot of money.

But Nonno also had a seedier side to his personality that my mother never told me about. My uncle told me that Mamma had been struck as a child and ridiculed for being too tall, too skinny, too anything. I can just imagine the kind of abuse that occurred at home. When I asked her about this one day, she told me that Nonno had a bad side to him and that I should not dwell on it. He was a good provider, and that is what she will always remember about him. "Basta!" (enough) she would shout at me when I kept asking questions about how she was treated as a child. How many memories was she shutting out?

I decided to call her back another day. After all, it was 7:00 p.m. in New York and too late to reach her in Italy. As I had hoped, the second message on the machine was from Robin, asking me if I wanted to catch some dinner that night. My heart fluttering in magnificent gratification, reminding me of the feeling I have before my plane lands in Italy, I searched my jacket pockets for the slip of paper that contained the valuable telephone number. It never fails: sacred things are always found in the last pocket to be checked or the last drawer to be opened. I was frazzled by the time I found it.

I punched in her number and waited.

"Hello," a strong voice answered.

"Hi, Robin? This is Jean from rugby. How you doing?" I said nervously.

"Oh," she hesitated slightly, as if realizing that she was doing something wrong. "Thanks for calling me back. How is your knee feeling?"

"It's a little swollen."

"Are you going to see a doctor?"

"No," I said stoically. "It's nothing serious. I think I just hyper extended it, or something. It will be better in a week."

"That's good to hear. You want to grab some dinner tonight? I have to run into the office to finish a couple of things on this proposal I'm working on. How about ten o'clock?"

"Where should we go?" I asked.

"How about we meet in the West Village at Marion's Eggplant Monster? It's on West Tenth off of Seventh Ave. It's cozy. If not, we can get some Chinese."

"Marion's sounds good, Robin. I'll see you there at ten. Let me run so I can get my work done."

"Look forward to seeing you later, Jean."

"Bye."

We hung up together.

Chapter 2

I put on a flowery surfer shirt and tight black jeans. My teeth were flossed, my underarms shaven (I do this only on first dates), my hair pulled back in a slick, wet bun. I sprayed on some Giorgio Armani for Men Cologne and a little Magie Noire behind the ears. I found this to be a seductive combination. She wouldn't know what hit her.

At 9:30 I took the elevator down to the lobby and walked out the door onto 114th Street. It was warm and muggy, and my jeans, though very sexy, were a bit too heavy for this day. The Columbia neighborhood was filled with people who were there only for the summer. I could tell by their eager demeanor and wondrous eyes. They sat at grungy sidewalk cafes, conversing loudly while smoking cigarettes. As if they were taking notes for some kind of sociology study, they looked around intently and spoke to the homeless people. They were excited to learn about how this multicultural community functions. This is New York City in all its splendor, they thought. They were content because they could leave all this behind, like a long day at the dentist's office. On the other hand, I could easily pick out the New Yorkers because they wore their usual downtrodden look of permanency.

The train was packed. Young Hispanic women dressed in white, black, and red held on to their boyfriends. Handsome boyfriends looked straight ahead, putting last minute touches on the form of their hair. A group of young African-American kids were yucking it up in the corner. A homeless man was prone on the bench. I stood in the corner closest to the conductor's booth. Though I occasionally had to move over to let somebody walk by, I had a good view of the proceedings in the car from here. A steady stream of people with grins on their faces moved passed me. There must be something particularly distasteful in the next car, a half-crazed outpatient or an odorous person.

I got out at 14th Street and proceeded to look for a place to buy some flowers and a bottle of champagne. I was on a mission: I wanted to show Robin that a woman could wine and dine a woman as well as any man could. At the Korean market on the corner, I bought a bouquet of yellow and violet flowers. Because flowers sold in the city are so far removed from their natural habitats, they are just colors.

At the liquor store, I told some guy behind the bulletproof window to get me a chilled bottle of their cheapest, finest champagne. He complied and handed me a bottle of André.

"This will do," I said and gave him $6.57. One day, far in the future, I'll have a real job and be able to afford some Moët. The things an adult must give up while in graduate school. Robin was making about $100,000 a year in a high-powered architect job. She had monetary freedom, but no time to enjoy it.

After circling the block a couple of times because I was early, I arrived at the restaurant at the desired time of 10:05. One should never get to a date too early. You don't want to appear overanxious. Robin was not there, so I pulled out a copy of Marge Piercy's latest from my fanny pack and began to read in the dim light of the street. If she finds me reading while waiting for her, she'll think I have a life apart from her, which I didn't because she was my latest obsession. Fifteen minutes passed—no glimpse of her. I started to get a bit irritated. Perhaps she forgot our appointment; she couldn't find the place. She got hit by a car. It was all over.

Robin jumped out of a cab at 10:35.

"I'm really sorry, Jean. I got hung up at work. My secretary got my instructions all wrong, and I had to go in and edit the proposal myself."

I pretended that I was fine.

"Don't sweat it. I was reading Marge Piercy." I put the book back in my trusty fanny pack. "I really like it. Do you know her stuff?"

I followed her into the dimly lit restaurant. She smelled like Zest deodorant soap, my favorite kind. Her hair was shiny. The V-necked T-shirt she was wearing certainly did her breasts justice. We took the table by the fireplace.

I couldn't take my eyes off her. Her neck was long and dark; her green eyes sparkled in the candlelight. I was a goner and would be with her that night.

"How's school?" She started the conversation.

"I'm taking my oral exams in two weeks and starting to prepare my syllabus for the coming semester."

"What do you teach?"

"Thinking about Music, a required course for all undergraduate students. It's equivalent to Music Appreciation. I teach them a little about the elements of music—rhythm, tempo, instruments—and then go through a rigorous survey of western music from Gregorian chant to Philip Glass, with an occasional woman thrown in."

"I wish I had taken a course like that in college. I was too busy with design and business courses to think about anything musical," she admitted.

I grabbed my chance to show-off. "I spend the first couple of days with the class trying to ease their minds about the syllabus and convincing them that the semester won't be so bad. Mozart and Beethoven's music carries with it an enormous amount of societal baggage. Kids think that they are dumb because they don't know anything about Bach. Isn't it true that we use music to determine a person's intelligence? If you prefer heavy metal to Bach, you are stupid, but if you like Mozart over Elvis, you are educated." I stopped because I realized I was going into my professorial lecture mode.

Robin seemed interested in this line of reasoning and asked me what kind of music I preferred.

"That's a tough question. Right now I'm rebelling against classical music in general. I can't listen to Schubert string quartets, Mozart symphonies, or even my favorite selections of Chopin pieces that I used to perform as a kid. Their music has come to symbolize white patriarchal hegemony. I'm afraid I can't get around it."

She seemed perplexed.

"How do you teach it then?"

"I try to focus on the various meanings of the music. I ask the class why they think Handel's *Messiah* is so popular. How has it become part of the popular consciousness?"

"I remember they played it at my high school graduation," Robin reflected.

The skinny waitress interrupted us to ask whether we wanted anything to drink.

Robin requested a business-womanly Scotch and soda, while I opted for a Coors Light, the beer of champion lesbians. I'm not exactly sure why the lesbian community embraces this brand—what with all the accusations of gender discrimination against the company.

Robin   hesitated   a   second   to   find   her   place   in   the conversation.

"The father of a friend of mine used to sing the 'Hallelujah' Chorus every Christmas Eve for the family. Let me think. . . . I also remember hearing it on some car commercial or another."

"See how it has become so utterly mainstream, whereas a more interesting piece like Stravinsky's *Rite of Spring* will forever remain on the periphery of culture. There is something relaxing about Handel. It doesn't challenge conceptions about what music should sound like. The heavenly connections help too. It's not threatening the way a lot of music is. Just think about the incredible outrage people feel over rap music. The guy writing for the *Times* believes that rap music caused the stampede last month at City College."

"Rap promotes violence; kids should not listen to it." Robin managed to get a word in edgewise.

We debated the topic a bit further—I was thoroughly enjoying this conversation. She was a good listener.

The waitress returned to take our dinner order. We asked her for another minute and began to study the menu.

"Do you recommend anything?" I asked.

"I usually get the grilled chicken and mushrooms. The entree comes with a fresh house salad. The pastas are nice too." I never eat spaghetti in restaurants in New York because I can make it better at home. What with an Italian mother! Pasta in New York always has too much sauce, and the noodles are generally overcooked because they are precooked. Plus a plate of pasta should realistically cost no more than four dollars. Restaurants charge up to twelve for a plate: ridiculous. I did not explain all this to Robin. It was too whiney for a first date.

"I'll have the rigatoni with pesto sauce," she told the patient waitress.

"I'll take the grilled chicken à la Marion," I said and beat the

waitress to the punch by telling her that Italian dressing would
be fine for the salad. I think Robin liked me.

"Phil likes Vivaldi," she volunteered. Phil was her boyfriend.
I'm not quite sure why she brought *him* up. Maybe she had to
remind me of her predicament.

"Really?" I came down to reality. "What else does *he* like?"
I asked.

"Jimi Hendrix, Radiohead, that kind of stuff." She realized that
she had changed the direction of the conversation. Don't most
women usually sit around and talk about their boyfriends?

For a brief instant, I remembered that Robin was not a dyke.
Not only was she not a dyke, she was involved with someone
else.

"Martha and I listen to a lot of chick music: Suzanne Vega,
Joni Mitchell, Tracy Chapman. I don't really like the Indigo
Girls that much."

The food came, and we talked about how it tasted and asked
politely if the other wanted a bite. I never understood this form
of pleasantry because I did not get much satisfaction from
eating a bite of food from another person's plate. I wonder how
she would react if I just started chowing down without asking.

"Tell me something about what you do. Did you always know
that you wanted to be an architect?"

"My Dad's in the business, and it just felt like the right thing
to do. To tell you the truth, I'm not happy with the kind of work
I do now. Most of it involves managing architects who design
bank lobbies. The work is somewhat interesting—the design
part, that is. But I do so little of that now. I recently helped put
together a huge deal in London for a new bank branch there. It
took me two years to get the British government to approve my
team's drawings to remodel a building. I also won a fellowship
to study at Harvard a couple of years ago. I studied Palladian

architecture."

Despite the fact that I had always been warned about going out with an architect (because of their weird work habits and persnickety personalities), I found this conversation to be very interesting. She was enthusiastic about discussing her projects, and at that particular moment, I could not understand why my piano teacher had categorically (a word that crept into mainstream parlance after the Clarence Thomas–Anita Hill debacle) stated that I should never marry an architect. Maybe they weren't all bad—I hoped.

She then explained that she made a shitload of money, with which she bought a condo in Manhattan. I was impressed. She was a grown-up with a big salary and her own place. I was used to associating with graduate school adolescents, who still asked their folks for money and ate a bagel and yogurt every day at lunch to save a couple of bucks.

"Tell me more about your family," I said. It must be an Italian thing. I always feel that somebody cares about me when they ask me about "the family."

"My sister Valerie died in a skiing accident." She stopped. "She was competing in the downhill event at Lake Placid when she lost control of her skis and smashed her head against the ice. She died two days later of massive brain injuries."

My God, I thought to myself. I suddenly felt sick to my stomach. I have no clue about how to act when someone informs me of a personal tragedy. My first impulse is to try to make it better. That's fine when it concerns something innocuous, say, like a D- minus on the big physics exam, or getting cut from the basketball team. But death? My grandma is the only person I ever knew who died, and she did it in Italy. Mamma never talked about it, and my stupid life just continued to drag on.

In a clumsy voice I asked, "How old was she?"

"Nineteen. My mother went into shock after she heard the news. She would not go into the room where her body lay crumpled and trembling. Dad just came out looking defeated. He made me ask the doctors if there was any hope."

"That must have been excruciating," I murmured under my breath.

"I'll never forget those last agonizing hours." A brief pause. "Here's a picture of her." She went into her wallet and took out a picture of a blond kid.

"She worked in Palo Alto one summer. She is pretty, isn't she?"

"Yes," I nodded.

"She was sophomore in college, majoring in biology. She loved to look at bugs."

I didn't know what to ask next. There is something dangerously appealing about seeing someone you are attracted to in distress. I wanted to throw my arms around her, say it would be OK. From that point on it was clear that she needed me. Or, in retrospect, was it I who needed her?

"When did the accident happen, Robin?"

"Six years ago in February. It was a viciously cold day. The snow had turned into a slick pane of ice, and ice drooped from the trees. I waited with Phil at the bottom of the hill. The loud speaker called out that Valerie Winter, number 54, from the University of Vermont, was on the course. We waited for her to break through the last line of trees, when, suddenly, at a speed of close to 40 miles per hour she lost control and veered off into the pines. There was a hush in the crowd. After what seemed like hours, we saw paramedics ski down to where she had disappeared. A helicopter appeared in the horizon and landed precariously on a flatter part of the course. Phil and I started to make our way up the icy slope. Five minutes into the climb, we saw the helicopter take off. They took Valerie to a hospital in Burlington, Vermont. It has a world-renowned head trauma unit.

"The doctors operated immediately. They drilled a small hole into the base of her skull to alleviate the pressure from a clot that had formed after impact. Apparently, she had lost her balance on a bump, flipped back on the heels of her skis, and smacked the back of her head on the ice. The force and position of the fall caused massive injury." Robin presented the facts to me methodically and unemotionally.

"She lived for two days on life-support."

I wasn't feeling hungry anymore and began pushing the chicken around the edges of my plate.

"It's something you never get over. Mom has completely stopped socializing, and Dad works eighty hours a week. It's torn us apart."

Nothing I could say could ever compare to this type of tragedy. It would only be much later that I'd realize she was using it to manipulate me.

Robin changed the subject to rugby. We talked about our last game, the score she made, and our crazed Irish coach, who was kicked off the field for disputing a silly call.

"He's an embarrassment," Robin said. "I can't stand it when he starts with that stuff: I'm Irish, and you know nothing, only how to eat popcorn."

I did not admit that I found that part of him charming. I loved his thick accent and Irish-centric thinking. His shenanigans seemed harmless to me. They reflected his insecurity about being a first-generation immigrant who still had a foot on the other side of the ocean. Just like my mother. When she was in Italy, she argued with friends that food tasted better in the U.S. When she was in New York, she said that food was not good, not like in Italy, where they had delicious bread, cheese, and vegetables.

"He was pretty annoying, I guess. But we played well any way."

As the waitress took our half-eaten meals away, I asked her for another round of drinks. Robin was starting to get tipsy.

"Jean, when did you first know you were gay?"

"I didn't come out until I was nineteen. Before that I had lots of crushes and infatuations and certainly no boyfriends. The first time I can remember having feelings for the same sex was in second grade."

"That young?"

"I was attending P.S. 89 in Queens. I loved my teacher, Miss Levinson, because she was kind and wore short, powder-blue dresses. She had a great sixties-style bob like Elke Sommer. I wanted to be near her so much that I spent most of my time following her around the classroom. One day while I was running right behind her to keep up, she suddenly turned around. My face—I was about three feet tall then—landed smack on her skirt, somewhere around her uterus. A surge of sexual delight swept across my entire body. A huge grin appeared on my face. This was heaven."

Robin laughed.

"You don't believe me?" I playfully shoved her shoulder. "That's when I knew I was different."

"What if you don't really have a preference? I used to have crushes on girls in high school, but I never did anything about it. It just didn't seem right. I didn't lose my virginity until I was twenty-four."

"Where did you meet Phil?"

"When I was still living in Pittsburgh. We worked in the same office. We've been through a lot together. He has been with me through some of the bad times and the good times. We have never lived together because I feel that somehow, something is missin."

My heart trembled with excitement. This could only mean one thing: she's gay.

"We have an open relationship. I tell him about the other guys I've been with, he says nothing and waits for me to marry him."

"I guess this means you have never been with a woman?"

"I've thought about it but never found the right opportunity."

This was my chance. I was mad about her, and she probably would sleep with me. I finished the beer and paid the waitress. We stumbled into the street.

"What do you want to do?" I asked.

"This is your part of town, you decide."

Have you been to a woman's bar before?"

"I went a couple of times when I was in college with some girls on the team. "

We walked under the short, shady trees of Jane Street.

"You haven't told me anything about Martha. What is your status? Are you still together?

I did not want to blow it and opted for: "Kind of. She's going to school in Boston."

"So you have a long distance relationship?"

"I don't know. I don't want to think about it. It upsets me too much." What a cop-out, I thought. I should have just told her the truth: I'd break up with Martha as soon as Robin broke up with Phil. That was my tacit deal with her. After all, I was in love.

We turned the corner onto Seventh Avenue, the unofficial division between gay and straight Greenwich Village. On hot nights, the street is filled with an intriguing mix of gays looking for bars and straights going to the theater, a jazz club, or an overpriced Mexican restaurant. Robin seemed comfortable with the whole scene, something I still had not mastered. Each time I walked down Seventh Avenue, I hoped that I wouldn't run into any of my students.

As on most Saturday nights, Nannie's was packed with women. I held the door open for my date and made my way past the imposing bouncer, who wore tattoos and a mustache. My first thought was to imagine what she must be like in bed. Would she strap me down, rip my clothes off, and burn me with a cigarette? Would I ask for more? My ex-girlfriend Sandy, the one with the insatiable sexual appetite, once told me that she used to dream about what anyone she ever met would be like in bed. Kind of a fun game.

Loud, politically correct music blared as women tugged on cigarettes. Colorful videos reflected off of dangling earrings. We found a corner of the bar and sought out the bartender for more drinks.

"Eleven fifty," she said as she placed the drinks on white napkins. She did not look at us.

"Wow." I couldn't help myself. Graduate-student reality suddenly escaped through my voice.

Sensitive to my distress, Robin picked up the tab. "Don't worry, Jean, I've got this one."

We stood close together and drank our ridiculously expensive drinks. Now I can show her what it would be like to be with a lesbian. I grabbed her left hand and immediately felt a reaction in the vicinity of my underwear. She did not move away from me or seem particularly appalled by my awkward come-on. Instead, she began to massage the hair on my forearm. She was gentle. I wonder if she does this to her boyfriend. The thought of that turned me on some more. I slowly made my way up to her shoulder, touching each inch of her arm and biceps. Chicks love that.

"Want to dance?" I interrupted our foreplay.

"Sure," she responded with a slight tremble in her voice.

We left our drinks on the bar and pushed our way passed young and old dykes.

"I usually don't like to dance unless I'm really drunk, Jean. I'm too self-conscious."

"Let the music move you."

I grabbed her by the waist and started doing my hip rotation move. Chicks usually fall for that. My hips gyrating, I move closer and closer to my prey until she can't do anything but hold on for dear life.

"You're a good dancer."

"So are you. I'm surprised you get so uptight about it. You can really move."

My favorite song by En Vogue came on, and I was transformed. I was John Travolta in *Saturday Night Fever* and showed off some of my fancier moves, complete with spins, dips, and jumps.

"You remind me of my first boyfriend," Robin smiled.

"Really?" I was puzzled. She had truly insulted me. I went back to a more conservative style.

When the song ended, I took Robin's hand and led her back to the safety of our drinks.

"I've never danced like that before," Robin mused. "Whenever I go to a straight place, I'm always so conscious of my body movements and the way men look at me. When I move too much, it's an invitation for them to be with me. I can be much freer here."

I didn't understand her point but nodded anyway.

"Let's dance some more," Robin said, grabbing my hand.

This time she was more relaxed. We watched two hot African-

American women weave their bodies around each other. Next to us, two women were bobbing up and down, their thighs rubbing into a smolder. Robin reached for my hand and placed it gently on the side of her hip. As the drum mix raged in the background, she raised her arms above her head and began to sway from side to side. I was witnessing a discovery of sensuality. We were part of the mass of dancers, each sweating to the thumping music. I was getting highly aroused.

We danced for hours. Each song made us more excited, and the taste of freedom made us yearn for more. Like Korean Shamans, who perform exorcisms in rooms filled with women, lesbians were exorcising the evil oppressive spirits from our society. Women's bars provide much more than a place to socialize. They are safe havens for women to experiment, to try roles that are denied us. This may be ordering a drink, leading a dance, gyrating to the music, chatting with a pal, making a move on someone you find attractive. No wonder straight women get so confused when they spend time with lesbians. They wonder, "Am I gay or am I free?"

Robin took my hand to see what time my digital watch read. 3:30 a.m. I nodded to her. We should go.

We walked by the long bar with drunk lovers still there because they were either having an illicit affair or lived with their parents.

Outside, Robin looked into my eyes.

"Please come home with me, Jean," she said sweetly.

"I can't think of anything I'd rather do."

We jumped into a cab that was waiting for lesbians outside the club. A strange, skinny man seated on a bed of yellow and brown beads kept a watchful eye on the rearview mirror as we sped up Madison Avenue to Robin's studio on East 91st Street. He waited for us to begin getting into each other's pants or kiss or something.

"So," I broke his concentration, "where are you from?"

"Russia," he said bitterly disappointed.

"My grandparents are from Riga. Do they have lesbians there?" I was drunk.

"What?" he asked. Robin shoved my side.

"Women who prefer to be with other women." I said slowly.

"I don't know. I've never known any."

My head started to spin, and I was feeling slightly nauseated. I probably shouldn't have had that last shot of Tequila. The bright streetlights blurred by us, and our horny Russian cab driver accelerated to 60 mph in five seconds and slammed on the brakes to stop at the light.

"I don't feel too well, Robin."

She held my hand and put her arm around my shoulder.

"Just another ten blocks."

My attention fuzzy, I hoped that I wouldn't puke the way I did on my first date with Martha.

Robin paid the driver, and we stumbled up two steps into the lobby of the building. The doorman said hello as Robin led me to the elevator. She lived on the fifth floor of this new building that housed other young urban professionals. She fumbled through her fanny pack for the keys and opened the door into a spacious living area.

"Let me get you some water," Robin offered in a comforting tone. "You'll feel better."

"I'm feeling better already. I think it was sitting in the cab with that mad Russian. How do you feel?"

"OK. I drank a little too much."

She handed me the glass of water and watched me drink. "I had a great time tonight," she said as she sat next to me on the couch.

"Me too. I haven't met someone I like to spend time with in a long time. I really like you."

I ran the fleshy part of my hand down the side of her face.

"You are beautiful," I told her as the energy level rose again. My labia were starting to burn with pleasure.

I turned my body toward hers, placed my hand slightly behind her neck, and kissed her in the shadow of her chin. She sighed. My mouth slowly made its way to her thick lips. They were so soft. I carefully inserted my tongue, exploring her smooth teeth and fleshy gums. She tasted good.

She reached for the top button of my blouse and slid her hand down the back of my shirt.

"You have a really strong back. Not to mention those legs. I used to get so distracted during our games. Instead of watching the ball, I'd watch your quadriceps ripple."

This kind of talk is music to my ears because I always felt self-conscious as a child about my body. Mamma told me I was too masculine. Girls at school made fun of me because "Jean plays basketball like a boy."

She took off my shirt and began. For someone who had never had a lesbian encounter before, she was confidently doing all the right things. She slowly lowered her head.

"That's wonderful, Robin." I assured her and myself.

"I'm so into you," she sighed. "I never imagined how powerful the feelings could be."

She slowly raised her head, grabbed my hand, and led me to her bedroom. We made love until the sparrows chirped and the morning light filtered into the room.

Chapter 3

The alarm sounded at 11:00.

"Jean, I'm sorry, but I have to go to the office to work on the Sun River project," Robin said matter-of-factly.

She jumped out of bed and into the bathroom. I heard the shower running. Reality hit Robin in the face, like a rush of cold water. What was she doing with this woman? What about Phil? Was she falling in love?

I lay perplexed on my stomach in the next room. She had assumed her professional architect demeanor in an instant.

"Let's at least get something to eat before you go," I pleaded. The energy of the previous night had disappeared. She treated me like a long lost friend whom she never really liked.

"I can't. The preliminary plans have to be on my boss's desk by five today. He's coming in from the Hamptons just to look at them."

I was crushed. We had spent a glorious evening together, we had shared the most intimate parts of our bodies, and now she was leaving me. I jumped out of bed over to my clothes, still soaking from sex and sweat.

When she walked out of the bathroom she asked me, "Don't you want to take a shower?"

"No thanks. I've got things to do myself [a lie]. My exam is in two weeks," I replied. Being of Italian descent, I never felt particularly dirty because I did not take a shower first thing in the morning. This horrified many of my American friends.

She hesitated. "Let's go get a bagel and some orange juice at the market. It's on the way to the subway." She compromised. "You smell good, Jean, like cigarettes, beer and love." She teased me. She put her arms around my waist and squeezed me tight.

I kissed her for the first time that morning.

We walked out into the light of a cloudy September day. The city is sleepy on Saturday mornings, and remnants of late-night partying cover the sidewalk.

Unexpectedly, she slipped her hand into mine.

"Robin, you can't do that. What if someone sees us—the doorman, somebody from work, a crazed neighbor? You have to be careful. People can be very cruel." My homophobia came to the forefront in the guise of protecting her.

"What are they going to do, kill us?" She began to swing my arm back and forth.

I had never held my lover's hand in public before. What an exquisite feeling! It felt like the first time I heard Brahms' Violin Sonata in G Major—the most beautiful piece of music ever composed. I kicked myself for spending thirty years of my life never knowing about such marvelous freedom. It only took me two blocks to get used to holding her hand. From that point on, I never wanted to let it go. Never.

I delighted in every move we made in the grocery store. I kissed the back of her head as she leaned down to pick an onion bagel out of the bin. She stroked my neck as I reached for some orange juice in the fridge. I put my hand in her pants pocket as she paid the cashier. She put her arm around my waist as we walked around to find a good place to eat. I was madly, hopelessly in love.

We walked to Central Park and sat on a green bench. Joggers and bikers whizzed by us. Huge guys with baseball bats and jockstraps worn on the outside of their pants gave us looks. Two women smiled at us.

"Here, Jean." She handed me the juice. "Do you want an onion or plain bagel?"

"Plain, please. What kind of spread is on it?"

"Just plain cream cheese—isn't that what you wanted?"

"Fine." At this point, she could have given me yams with chunks of coconut, the only two things in the world that I won't eat, and I would have relished them.

We did not speak much that morning. I was burning to ask her how she felt about making love to me. Did she enjoy it? Would we do it again anytime soon? Was she thinking about her boyfriend? Instead we talked about the Yankees and how much we liked Derek Jeter. Though I could not admit it to myself, something was very wrong. She thanked me for a great time, said she'd call, and hailed a cab. I was alone and desperate without my love at noon on a Saturday. This was not the usual case of lesbian merge.

I walked across Central Park at 97th Street. The softball fields were crammed with yuppies and their picnic accessories purchased at Conran's. On the fringes, men dressed in colorful clothing played soccer as their girlfriends waited patiently. A softball rolled toward my foot, and I bent down to pick it up. I delivered a hard throw back to the first baseman. My dad taught me how to throw like a boy when I was young. The only problem with knowing how to throw like a boy is that you have to modify it for sexist situations. This is because it makes certain individuals nervous. When I was sixteen, I had an ice cream with a handsome Italian boy and found myself flipping him the keys to his house underhanded so as not to startle him with the wind-up overhand toss I usually used with a friend. The underhand toss must also be accompanied by a silly smile and hands to the face. Overhand = boys; underhand = girls. God how I hated this world, sometimes.

Because I had envisioned a long passionate weekend with Robin, I had no plans for this Saturday afternoon. Saturday afternoons were usually spent with lovers in bed or doing the laundry. Martha and I like to stroll down West Broadway looking at the art galleries. Sometimes we'd play softball with some other dykes. Today I was alone, and, to tell you the truth, I didn't know how to handle it. I felt uneasy in my heart, the place where I experienced most of my anxiety. How could somebody as madly in love as I was stand to be apart from the person she adored for more than a couple of hours? This was cruel and unusual punishment. Romeo could never live without Juliet for more than a couple of hours, Maria without her Tony, Martina without her Rita Mae. I was completely out of breath and irrational when I exited the park on the West Side.

I know. I will drive to Boston this afternoon and tell Martha a story. I'll say nothing about Robin, just explain to her that I wanted to break up because our relationship was stagnating and I needed to move on. She will certainly understand.

Robin was not on the beaten track of lesbian lovers in the tri-state area. Hell, she wasn't even gay. That would give me enough time to decide whether Robin and I might continue seeing each other. If it didn't work out, Martha is spared the sexy details. How considerate of me. Going to Boston made perfect sense, I said to myself as I walked to the nearest pay phone to call her. Pay phones in New York City are always occupied. The ones that aren't are broken. Either there is no dial tone or you place your quarter in and never get it back. Someone must cleverly jam the machines and come back later to retrieve her jackpot.

I waited about ten minutes for a Latino woman to get off

the phone with her boyfriend. He must have called her at that number. After several rings, Martha picked up the phone and sounded happy to hear from me.

"That's a long drive for just half a day," she pondered.

"I need to talk to you about something serious, and I don't want to discuss it over the phone."

"Are you all right?" She sound genuinely concerned.

"Yeah, I'm fine. We've got to get some things straightened out." (In retrospect, I wish I could have told her the truth. She might have been able to save me from the rest of this story.)

Her voice descended an octave. "I have plans for dinner with Donna tonight. I can meet you afterward."

"How's nine o'clock? I'll be at your dorm room at nine."

"Sounds good.

"Fine." (I'm in love, I thought to myself. I'm doomed.)

"Promise you'll drive carefully."

"Yes. See you tonight."

My eyes glazed over from lack of sleep, I made my way slowly up Broadway. Lists of fourteenth-century composers sprang into my consciousness, and I placed each one of them in a specific time and location. Guillaume de Machaut, the great French composer, was born around 1300 and died in 1377. Francesco Landini, the great blind Florentine composer, was born around 1320 and died in 1388. Robin, the greatest lover I had ever been with, who stroked the inside of my thighs as I dug my fingers into her wetness, was born in Pittsburgh. She pleasured me. She held my hand in public. Her father was an architect; she had a boyfriend, a brother, and a sister. This was pointless.

My parents' Volvo was parked in a garage on 125th Street. They put it there because if they left it on the street it would be stolen or vandalized. Americans had lost the freedom to park the car in front of their homes. We were also slowly losing the right to govern the fate of our own bodies.

I had cracked up the previous family car five years ago after a violent fight with an ex-lover. One afternoon, I came back to her house early from a summer job and found her in bed with my basketball coach. Shrieking in horror, I proceeded to slam all her dishes on the floor one by one. With her pleading for me to stop, saying that it wasn't what it seemed, I moved to the glasses and threw each one against her wall. The two of them couldn't come near me because they would have cut up their feet.

I had plenty of dish- and glass-smashing experience in my family to know that it was an effective method of producing shame. After finding out that he was not inheriting the land underneath the Mont Blanc from my grandfather, Uncle Davide picked up his dinner plate filled with spaghetti and flung it against the family tree. My mother screamed and Grandma ran into the kitchen for cover.

"*Sei un bastardo*," Davide yelled in a baritone.

My father grabbed my arm and led me out of the house, explaining that greed only leads to violence.

"You should never value material possessions more than people," he said shaking his head. He then took me to the local *gelateria* for an ice cream, where he proceeded to argue with the vendor over the inordinately high price of his product. I stood by licking my cone, embarrassed by the whole scene.

After smashing all the dishes, I decided to drive up to Cold Springs, New York, a quaint tourist trap on the Hudson River. The sun was bright as I made my way off the highway exit in Ossining. I'd take 9W passed the GM plant, up the mountainous road to my destination. The car stereo blaring, the sun beaming through the glass, Debbie in bed with coach, wishing my pain away, I didn't see the stop sign and was hit broadside by a nice young woman driving a beat-up Dodge. My car spun around three times before it rammed into the stop sign. A cop, who had been waiting on the corner to catch drivers who did not stop at the sign, peered through the shattered glass.

"Are you OK?"

"Yeah," I said a bit dazed. Nothing was seriously wrong with my body. I just felt like I wanted to die. Why hadn't I?

As curious neighbors came to check out the scene, they placed me in the back of the police car. They told me that I had gone through the stop sign, as if I didn't know. I had left my license at home—so that was another violation—and I was driving without my glasses. To add insult to injury, Howard Stern's radio show blared in the back seat. The cops dropped me off at the nearest train station, and I waited for the express to New York City.

My drive to Boston proceeded smoothly. I traversed all the towns I could live in if my parents were Protestant with money: Greenwich, Old Saybrook, Westport, and Newport. This was a world I could never been privy to. This was a world inhabited by our president and most of the government, especially the Senate. No wonder we have race relations problems in the U.S.: our elected officials have as much understanding of Middle America as I have of Connecticut.

A large, multicolored Burger King appeared on the horizon, and I pulled over to get something to eat. I parked next to vans that were filled with screaming children and pissed-off mothers.

I had to pee and contemplated my patented procedure of using the ladies' room without having to come into contact with anyone else's germs. First, I wash my hands. Then, I take toilet paper and wipe the toilet seat and put a fresh piece of paper around the seat. Then, I do my business. After that I wash my hands at the sink. Now the tricky part: how to get out of the bathroom without touching any of the surfaces with my clean, antiseptic hands? While leaving the faucet on, I go over to the paper towel dispenser and grab one. If by chance a towel is not hanging at my disposal, I use my forearm to push on the lever to crank down another one. I then move quickly to the running faucet and turn it off with the hand that has the paper towel. Paper towel still in hand, I turn the knob of the ladies' room and place the towel in the nearest trash receptacle. (If there is no doorknob, I fling the paper towel in the bathroom receptacle and push open the door with my shoulder.)

I did not attempt such a difficult maneuver in this Burger King bathroom. I'd save that for a more special occasion. The lines for the food were fairly short, and I had to choose fast, before a busload of kids from New Jersey invaded the space.

"How can I help you today?" an unusually attractive teenager asked me.

"I'd like a Whopper with cheese, French fries, and a medium Coke, please. Is that part of the special super-combo meal deal?"

"Yes, ma'am." I feel so relieved when people get my gender correct. "Will that be all for you today?"

"Could you give me extra ketchup?" I was salivating at this point. How embarrassing to salivate at the thought of a Whopper. Remember when those things first came out in the seventies?

I thanked the girl, wondered if she liked girls, and sat down at the furthest table. Like the seats in concert halls, the seats at fast food joints are generally nailed to the floor so that everyone eats their food in particularly restrictive directions. I found one that looked out onto the busy parking lot.

This Whopper was weak. The bread was stale and the burger was lukewarm. I should have asked for another one. Rather, I settled for the one I had and snarfed it down with my fries and a splash of Coke. Unsatisfied with my meal, I walked to the parking lot and drove over to the gas area to fill up the tank. A nice looking guy in blue overalls asked me what he could do for me today.

"Fill it up with premium, sir, and could you check the oil?" I always had the oil checked when I went on drives that lasted more than two hours. Dad told me that the engine could melt without oil. That's what happened to all our Fiats.

"Oil's fine, Ma'am. That will be thirteen dollars." I handed him one-tenth of my weekly paycheck from teaching in graduate school and sped off into the twilight. Provided there was no traffic along the route, I figured I'd be in Boston in two hours.

I found an appropriately sappy radio station so that I could dream about Robin. A wave of passion surged through my body as I tried to imagine the next time we would be together. As a Rod Stewart song blared, I thought about penetrating her with my hand and touching her with my mouth. She was so incredibly sexy. I should give her a call at the next stop. Tell her how much I enjoyed the previous night, how I would give my heart and soul to her. My life meant nothing without her (it also meant nothing with her). A car honked at me because I had drifted into the left lane. I gave the guy an apologetic wave and drifted back into my daydream. Grandma would have given the guy the finger. She always drove in the middle of the road while eating pistachio nuts.

Martha's dorm at the Business School faced the Charles River. Time-honored ivy covered its walls, and lush green lawns separated the buildings. Blond women walked about the campus as their checkered-jacketed dates discussed the latest case to be analyzed. An occasional nonwhite crossed campus. The Business School's gymnasium sparkled in the night.

My favorite story about Martha's first days at school involved this guy Greg, who dropped out of the program after three weeks. In the venerated main hall of HBS, Greg was called on to summarize a case about cat food supplies in pet stores. He clearly hadn't read the case—a cardinal sin for HBS—and tried to bullshit his way around the argument. As he was talking about this and that brand of cat food, the professor became more and more impatient with his obvious lack of respect for the topic and his classmates. After ten minutes of aimless meandering, the professor interrupted Greg and asked him to see him after class. In a booming voice Greg sat down in his seat and said, "Well, that about kills it." Conservative students looked at him in disbelief. Martha grinned. I thought this guy had incredible courage. He was probably an artist whose father paid for him to go to B-School. He was clearly a renegade freethinker.

I rang the doorbell at Martha's dorm and after two minutes, she came stumbling down the stairs.

"Hey," she hugged me in her strong arms.

"You look good—losing some weight, I see."

"I've just been incredibly busy. I have five classes a day. I stay up until one every night to get all the work done. Not much time to eat."

She walked me up two flights of stairs to her room. The place was a mess: dirty clothes stuck to the backs of chairs and books were strewn on the floor.

"It's good to see you, Jean. You're looking pretty skinny yourself. All that studying. Only two weeks before the big day. How do you feel?"

I panicked a little. The thought of the exam nauseated me.

"I've pretty much finished the bulk of my studying. I'm just reviewing things here and there."

"Are you hungry?"

"Yes. I stopped for a burger on the way, but I could really go for some better food."

"I'll take you to this great Thai place in Cambridge. It's my favorite."

"Sounds good, Martha." Martha showed me the way into this steamy, run-down bathroom.

"For Harvard Business School, this is pretty grim," I said."

"The shower is good though," she yelled back from the next room. My legs were shaking as I hovered over the bowl. Martha loved me, and I had to tell her that it was over. I took a shower to clean off last night's sex.

We walked across the Charles to Cambridge. Old professors on bicycles whizzed by us in the warm air. Joggers were out on late-night runs.

"Do you still run, Martha?" I made small talk.

"Nope, I play basketball with some women on Saturdays."

We did not say a word for several minutes.

I could not hold it back any longer. Thoughts of missing Robin drifted into my mind. "I need to tell you something." I led her over to a bench and grabbed her by the hand.

She paused. "Are you interested in somebody else?" She beat me to the punch.

"No, Martha," I lied.

"Are you telling me the truth?"

"Yes," I lied again. "Things have just not been good between us for the last couple of years. We don't touch each other in an intimate way. We don't have sex."

"We could see a therapist."

"No, no. . . ." I trembled. I had made up my mind to

dedicate myself to my new love, Robin. Like an alcoholic who desperately needs a drink, nothing could stand in my way from being with her. She was my obsession that would coddle my soul for the next months. I was terrified of failing my exams. My parents would never forgive me. "I think our relationship has been incredibly rewarding. I mean, I've never been as close to anybody as I've been to you. But in order to grow as a person, I need to be alone for a while. Understand who I am." I was really stretching reality now.

I have such good intentions when I break up. I knew she'd find somebody else within a matter of weeks.

"I need to start relying on myself for everyday pleasures. I can't keep making someone else the source of my life. Do you know what I mean?"

"Yeah, Jean. You've got to deal with your own neediness before you can really settle down."

I suddenly felt very vulnerable. "What do you mean? I'm not needy."

"You can't be by yourself. I always have to do things for you. Make calls, go shopping." She paused. "And you are homophobic."

Now she was pushing it.

I came from an eccentric family who loved me and let me bring my lovers back to the house whenever I wanted. Many parents disowned their children outright. Not my folks.

Martha pursued her point, "Your mother tells your brother not to hang out with homosexuals. Doesn't that say anything to you?"

My brother is an artist and comes in contact with many creative gays. "She just doesn't want him to catch something. She's concerned."

"What?" Martha was outraged. "You can't get AIDS from

casual contact."

"I know that. She is just worried. She worries about everything."

Martha got up off the bench and started walking back toward the B-school.

I followed her back across the dark Charles River. "Martha, I think that I just want to go home." I was drowning in my own pack of lies and needed desperately to get my head above water.

Even in the midst of an argument, Martha was forever thoughtful. "It's a long trip, Jean. Do you want to take a nap before you go?"

"No, I have to go." Without tears or supplication, she walked me over to the gray Volvo, hugged me, and whispered that she loved me. I figured she had somebody else.

"I'll tell you how the exam goes. I can't wait for the whole ordeal to be over."

We parted as friends. It was all so bizarre.

I needed to get into trouble because I was feeling so alone. I got off the highway in Danbury and drove ten miles west to the women's club my friend Chucky takes me to every time I visit her. Maybe she and her girlfriend, Treasure, would be there tonight. I figured I'd sit at the bar for a couple of hours, watch some suburban New England dykes dance, and get home late so that I could just fall asleep—exhausted. That way I wouldn't have to think about what I had just done.

I entered the club through the swinging screen door. A classy woman wearing a white T-shirt and jeans asked me for five dollars and stamped my hand with a purple asterisk. The place was packed with dancing couples on the right, and I made my way straight to the bar on the left. Squeezing between two women clearly in love, I got the attention of the softball-slinging dyke and asked her for my usual Bloody Mary. I'm not exactly sure why I like to order these at women's bars. After all, a Bloody is a morning or brunch kind of drink. Maybe it was something about the name of the drink itself. So female, so violent.

"Extra Tabasco, I like it hot." The woman to my right got up to dance, and I sat down in her seat.

"That will be four dollars."

I gave her five and told her to keep the change. The Bloody was cold, spicy, and strong. They make them best in New England. A larger woman sat down next to me and ordered a beer. Her glasses made her look more intelligent than she was, and I asked her where she was from.

"Darien," she replied.

"I'm from the City." People outside a sixty-mile radius of New York are usually quite impressed with this fact.

"Which city?" She seemed puzzled.

"New York. I'm sorry. I assume there is only one city on this planet."

She smiled. She told me her name was Vicky.

"What do you do?" I asked as the vodka started to kick in.

"I'm an account executive in a PR firm."

"What does that mean?" PR seemed such a nebulous business. Do they promote products? Advertise? I could never get it straight and told her so.

"We try to get information on TV about a product for free."

"Oh, that's right. Now I remember." I had an enemy from college who was doing that after she graduated.

"I like it pretty much. Sometimes it gets tedious, especially when I have to make a hundred phone calls to people asking them to put a story on. Generally I like it, though. What do you do?"

"I'm a graduate student at Columbia University." People usually got impressed at this point. I lost them after I described the musicology program I was in.

We ordered another drink. "Are you here alone?" she asked.

She told me about her last girlfriend, who had given her the boot. I told her about how I had extricated myself out of a perfectly loving relationship two months ago. I didn't want to scare her off by telling her it was really two hours ago.

When my favorite Prince song came on, I asked Vicky if she wanted to dance. She hesitated a little, put her drink down, and said what the hay. She moved from side to side in a fairly conservative manner. In my old age, I feel myself getting increasingly frustrated with the way we dance. We generally hold our elbows at our sides, arms swinging slightly. Our hips move slightly under our rather stiff torsos, with a little bit of shoulder action. In a duple beat, we move back and forth and sprinkle in an occasional full-circle spin. I wanted to dance like the "Fly Girls" on the show *In Living Color*, arms waving, frenetic bodies working up a real sweat. Instead, I mimicked my new friend and watched the video behind her.

We danced to four or five more tunes and walked back to the bar. I ordered her another beer and myself a Bloody. The bartender looked me straight in the eye.

"And a glass of water, please." I better take it easy if I intend to drive home.

"Have you ever picked up someone in a bar?" I asked Vicky.

"Nope. I generally come with a group of friends. I was feeling especially lonely tonight."

"I once went home with a doctor in the Navy. I met her at a straight wedding in Washington, D.C. She was the bride's ex-girlfriend. I was there with a friend. After the ceremony, she asked me if I wanted to get a drink and brought me to some small place on the coast where her military pals hung out. We had a few, and then she took me home. I guess that's as close as I ever got to being picked up in a bar." She seemed impressed. And I qualified my statement.

"I would rather fall in love with the person before I have sex with them. It makes the whole experience more rewarding." That seemed to make sense to her too. "I'm in love with an architect right now. We slept together last night. She has a boyfriend and works all the time." I stopped making sense.

"You shouldn't be sleeping with someone with a boyfriend. It's bad news. I did that once in college. She assured me that she would break up, but they just kept it on. She couldn't be alone. I was heartbroken."

I told her that my situation was different because I was certain that Robin would fall in love with me. It was just a matter of time before she relieved herself of the boyfriend. I was sure of it.

Vicky was not convinced and shook her head twice. I suppose I'd have to learn the hard way. We danced a couple more times. She took my hand and began to massage the inside of my arm. Though I wasn't particularly attracted to her physically, I thought that the event would make a good story to tell my friend Rachel. Rachel loved to hear about my make-out sessions. She dated guys now, but had had her share of experiences with women.

We walked away from the bar to a darker corner. Vicky began to kiss my neck, and I went along for the ride. We did not say a word. The alcohol acted as a buffer between Vicky and my reality. In my mind, I replaced her with Robin and then Martha and then back to Robin. My underwear was starting to get soaked. When she put her hand in my shirt she suddenly bit down hard on my lip and blood began to stream out of it. I was shocked. She grabbed my breast hard and began pinching my nipple. I didn't really know how to react to this aggression. In my drunken state, it felt pretty good, but at the same time, it felt pretty bad. Gathering my drunken wits, I shoved her as hard as possible and she landed against a row of bar stools.

"What the hell are you doing?" I yelled at her. She looked at me confusedly, but did not move. A smallish dyke with bright red lipstick ran over to Vicky to see if she was OK. The burly dark bouncer, who was summoned from her position next to the door, grabbed me and pinned me to the wall.

She stuck her face in the middle of mine and looked down at my bleeding lip. "There will be none of that S and M shit in this place. Get the hell out."

S and M, I wondered, is that what Vicky was up to? The bouncer took me by the arm and bent down to pick up Vicky. She led us to the door and, with an extra push, threw us out. We looked at each other, dazed.

"What the hell is the matter with you, Vicky?"

"I've been reading about S and M in *On Our Backs* and thought I'd try it. I'm piss drunk. I'm really sorry." She mumbled. "I'm really sorry. I've just been so out of it lately. How about something to eat?" Vicky asked. "You can't drive back to New York in the state you're in."

"Speak for yourself."

"There's a Friendly's just down the road. Let's get a Clambake Special."

The lights of the Friendly's could be seen in the distance, and we began to salivate. Despite all the things I hated about living in the suburbs, I loved the food. I became fixated on a meal of fried clams, French fries, and a Friendly chocolate shake. Vicky said she wanted a burger. We walked over to the first empty booth, far away from the drunken teenagers wearing black concert T-shirts. The meal came and went, as did the check that Vicky picked up, and we walked slowly back to the cars. We exchanged numbers and wished each other luck in our respective love affairs. My lip was swollen.

Chapter 4

The exam was a week away. By this point I had lost nearly twenty-five pounds and was down to sleeping just three hours a night. The rest of the time was not devoted to studying, but to watching TV. Every morning for the last three months, I had gone to the music library to dig up some treatise or another on medieval music and tested myself by reading it in its original language; this meant Latin, Italian, or French. I had managed to avoid having German on the exam, which was a good thing since I had to take the required German language exam three times before I passed. Though my Jewish grandmother said that German was a beautiful language when spoken correctly, I had something against the whole thing. Maybe it was the Nazi past. Perhaps it was all those K's, M's and N's. It was such a dark language, full of patriarchal declensions and hegemonic sentence structures. Not that I really understood this to be a fact. It just seemed that way to me.

Maybe it was because German soldiers occupied my mother's home in the Alps during World War II. Mamma told me that one day the family was sitting around the dinner table when there was a loud knock on the door, and a German commander demanded to come in. In terror, the kids ran into the other room as my grandfather tried to reason with the officer. The German demanded that the family pack and leave the premises immediately because he wanted to use the house for soldiers' quarters. He said that the house's position in the middle of the narrow mountain valley and its long balconies made it an ideal lookout. They would eventually put four huge black cannons on the balconies.

The Germans occupied the house for a full year. Mamma said the house stunk of beer, cigars, and urine. Imagine German soldiers sleeping in your bed. I get nightmares.

The doctoral exam tested this lowly graduate student's knowledge of a particular hundred-year period. I had to be familiar with all the primary and secondary literature of that era. That meant knowing the titles and composers of all the pieces, details about existing manuscripts, and any information about the instruments people played in the fourteenth century. In addition, I had to know all that was ever written about the subject, who the leading scholars were, and their stands on particular issues. For instance, American Joe Doctor so and so thought that Francesco Landini picked tomatoes in his garden, while Sir Musicologist from London believed that he harvested broccoli. Most of this was just the worst and besides did not teach you anything about how the music sounded. I just memorized an enormous amount of facts, all of which I would forget during a two-month period.

I figured I'd review my notes. No sense memorizing anything new. Like a filled-up floppy disk, my mind could not process new information. I saw Monica in the stacks. She had passed the big exam last year and had that condescending air typical of graduate students who had already aced a requirement.

"You're taking it next week, right?"

As if she didn't remember. She had seen me in that library five days a week all summer long while my parents and brother frolicked in Italy.

"It won't be long now." I felt sick.

"You want me to test you on anything?"

"Why don't you pick out a treatise in Latin. I'll try to translate it."

"Be back in a couple of minutes."

Monica was about thirty-seven. White roots sprouted beneath her stiff red hair. She was a medievalist too, studying French thirteenth-century theoretical treatises about melodic modes. She lived, breathed, and pooped graduate school. She once warned me not to seek the advice of a former Ph.D. student at Columbia because "I think she is a lesbian." Get a life.

Monica dealt with her ambiguous sexuality in a different way. Like many musicologists, she had none.

Monica finished her Ph.D. last spring and still hung around the music library. She could not find a job in the field because of the recession and did research daily to pass the time.

"Jean, I've found the perfect thing." She made me a Xerox of a document and placed it in front of me.

"Look at it carefully first. In the exam, they will want you to suggest the author of the excerpt, when you think it was written, and the gist of what he is saying. You may be able to find clues in the margins, the handwriting, or the size of the border."

I looked at it intently and thought, I can't believe I'm actually going through with this. I was never that smart—a B- student as an undergraduate, majoring in hangover relief. I only went to graduate school to get away from my tragically boring job at Alfa Romeo, where I was the inventory manager for their spare-parts division. I am basically a stupid person. My father used to introduce me to his colleagues with the words, "Here is my stupid daughter." He thought that was funny. I believed him.

"Monica, the way I see it," (I said these words to Joni Mitchell's "Free Man in Paris") "it looks French."

"Yes, it's in French, Jean. What else?"

She either didn't understand my humor, or she didn't know

Joni's song.

"Let's see, the handwriting. Hmm . . . the notes appear to be filled-in rather than white. They signify a later hand."

"Good, you're right."

"Late fourteenth-century, of course."

"Yes," she said in the same tone Marv Albert uses when the Knicks score a basket.

I felt very relieved. "Now, in the first paragraph, the author talks about watching two women bathing in a stream. Sounds very much like some of Machaut's musical poetry. This smut must be by Machaut, fourteenth-century composer for the kings of France."

"Right on. You'll have no problem with this exam, Jean." I still felt sick to my stomach.

I went into lecture mode. "These scantily clothed girls playing in water remind me of those disgusting videos on MTV. You know those old David Lee Roth videos where he pours water on women while ogling their breasts. Some things never change. The more I study fourteenth-century Italy, the more I realize that twentieth-century New York is very similar. The media succeeds in duping women and minorities into thinking that we all have it better than we had it back then. In reality, it is all the same." I continued after a breath.

"Women were warriors, saints, and politicians back then. We were writers and champion chess players and intellectuals. Now that we have a greater opportunity to join particular parts of the work force as teachers (though they tell us we can teach in universities, the tenure process for women is so discriminatory that few of us attain tenure with our mind and integrity intact), middle managers, lawyers, and doctors, some of our most basic human rights are restricted. Sexual harassment on the job, the 'glass ceiling,' and the 'mommy track' help to keep a woman's self-esteem low and confine us to a new ivory tower, where we're still at the mercy of men, like Boccaccio's women who are locked up by their husbands in the *Decameron*. Maybe we were better off in the nineteenth century, hanging around tea parties, playing the piano, and talking about poetry while our husbands killed each other over property or love. In some ways, we probably have lost as much freedom as we have gained.

"The corrupt media tells women that things are improving. Women can buy bigger cars and better washing machines with their own salaries. We can hire nannies to take care of the kids while we work. We can divorce our husbands and find new ones. There are major problems in all of this. Women are not accepted as professionals the way men are. We are still objects of desire in our flashy new Mercedes. We still have to get the wash done in the washing machines. Having a nanny raise your child takes away the joy of being a mother. We still can't win because it is still their game. As I see it, creating the illusion that women have it better than we used to accomplishes two things. First, it induces a certain guilty feeling in women by suggesting that men have sacrificed some of their own power to help us. Second, it keeps women from questioning the injustices of the system because we are under the false pretense that things are improving."

I was running out of breath. "What do you think, Monica?"

Not being much of a feminist, Monica nodded her head as a reflex action. I think that she stopped listening to me when it was clear that I would be focusing on a "woman's issue." The whole thing was too dangerous for her to consider. Her life was better spent speculating over the most authoritative version of some thirteenth-century theoretical passage that was found in three different versions in three different sources. I'd rather type telexes at Alfa Romeo than live an unexamined life.

Monica politely asked me if there was anything else she could help me with. I said no because I felt pretty confident about my abilities to bullshit about any text put in front of me. I was a master bullshitter. My professors showed me a certain respect when it came to my feminist viewpoints, and I figured that I could always impress them by extricating a feminist dialogue out of a fourteenth-century text. I was the only feminist graduate student or faculty member in the music division, and although I felt ostracized at times from the rest of my colleagues, they always came to me because I was the expert in such matters. Marginalization was accompanied by a certain amount of importance. "Go ask Jean; she's the feminist," I once heard a professor counsel a younger student.

I picked out some scores from the shelf and sat down at a cubicle. One volume contained songs by Lorenzo Masini, an Italian composer of the fourteenth century who specialized in writing dirty lyrics about voyeuristic men peering through trees to look at women bathing. I flipped through the pages to remind myself of some titles, "Monna Lapa, lift up your skirt; The grass beneath your legs grows in the shade" and my favorite, "Go finish the laundry, rain is coming." Medieval scholars have never remarked on these texts. Instead, male intellectuals (and many repressed female ones, who, in some cases, sleep with the male medievalists to get that big job) spend the bulk of their time deciding where the score was written, what type of pen the scribe wrote with, and what the most authentic text was. I suppose that there is certain validity to spending one's entire existence on this planet trying to determine whether the note in some obscure medieval piece was an A or an A-flat. My professor tried to convince me of this in our brainwashing introductory graduate seminar. I never bought it, and in five years of writing seminar papers, I never did any research that involved musical notation. Medieval women weren't taught notation.

We are transfixed by notation in Western society. What survives on the page is translated into what music sounds like. The easiest way to refute this silly tenet is to recall any experience you ever had playing rock-n-roll sheet music on the piano. I'll never forget going to parties as a teenager and being begged to play whatever was collecting dust on the person's piano. Jean, can you play Joni Mitchell? I have the music. Cringing, knowing that I was only dutifully trained to read Bach, Beethoven, and Brahms scores, I was lost when my classmates put a relatively simple Joni song sheet in front of me. Not that I couldn't play the right notes in the correct time, but I still sounded nothing like her recordings. She plays the guitar, shifts the tempo, adds vocal inflections and other instruments. My rendition of songs from *Court and Spark* were flat. My classmates were inevitably disappointed, and I generally stopped midway and played a lick from a Beethoven sonata. Except for an occasional odd girl, who was completely ridiculed in the high school like me, my peers were not impressed.

It was clear that I was having trouble concentrating that day. The exam was too close, and I was overloaded. Three days ago, I had called up Robin and told her that I couldn't see her or talk to her for ten days because I could not deal with any distractions prior to my exams. I would drive my parents' car over an embankment if I failed the exam because I had used up precious time dreaming about the way Robin smelled as I caressed the back of her neck with my tongue.

She got pretty upset when I asked her to lay low for a while. I had expected a different reaction, maybe one of sympathy and understanding. Instead, the next day she left two messages on my machine, the first asking me to call her back, the second asking me to spend the night. I wrote her a sweet card after the last message: "Robin, I think of you every minute of the day and long to be in your arms. I'll see you the moment I'm done." I didn't hear back from her.

I picked up my notes and flung them into my backpack. Forget this; maybe I'll go home and write a poem about her. I think that Phil was coming up from Pittsburgh this weekend. She'll forget I exist. Maybe she'll tell him about me. Doubt it. I decided to give Rachel a call and meet her for lunch.

Showered and blow-dried, Rachel was waiting for me in front of the coffee shop. She was wearing ripped jeans and a T-shirt from camp Ramah, the place she had worked as a counselor all summer.

"Hey, Bean." She hugged me, saying my nickname.

"Hey, Rach. Did I wake you up before?"

"Yeah, I was out late with Morris last night. Went down on each other."

"Yuck."

She knew how much the thought of sex with the opposite sex grossed me out and always gave me a little tidbit to start our time together. I shoved her playfully. She grinned.

"I can't understand how any woman in her right mind would ever suck a man's dick," I said in all seriousness.

"Come on. When you love someone you want to make them feel good, right? I really care about Morris."

I was not convinced. Penises stood for destruction and abuse. "I could never do it, Rachel." Whatever. My politics certainly did not make this world go round.

"So what's with this Robin?"

"I think she likes me. I told her to please give me a couple of weeks to pass my exams, and then I would see her. For some reason she didn't listen and called me again the same day. Do you think that it's some kind of fatal attraction thing?"

"She sounds scary." Rachel was forever kidding me.

"Come on, I'm being serious. I think that she can't live without me—already. She must be madly in love."

"Come on, Jean, you slept with her once. Why are you so frightened of her?"

"I don't really know. She has had such a sad life. You know, with her sister dying and everything. She works all the time. I think that she is desperate for love."

"Whatever you say. Let's decide what to have for lunch." Although there was a wide assortment of ethnic food on Broadway, from Japanese, to Greek diner, to pizza, to Chinese, Lebanese, and American, everything tasted pretty much the same: grimy. I opted for the usual slice at Happy Pizza.

The pizza place was filled with kids with blue and orange rings around their mouths from cheap sodas. I found a seat closest to the back mirror, near the mosaic picture of Naples' harbor. Rachel went to get the food. This was a good place to talk about sex because graduate students and faculty usually opted for more chic joints.

"Do you want some seasoning on your slice?" she yelled over the din.

"A little garlic, salt, and some red pepper."

Rachel placed a tray on the wooden table, holding two slices of regular pizza and two medium cokes.

"Tell me everything you did with her."

"We made passionate love at her place. I used that famous move I've been trying to teach you: one hand behind the back of the head, the other on the side of her face. Don't get too excited, Rachel, OK?"

"I could never do something like that. Women aren't that into me. You're the stud, the Martina. I'm the dud."

"You just need to practice a little more. You're really cute and loving, a great catch."

"Thanks for the encouragement. So then what happened?"

"She started undoing my shirt, and then she led me to her bedroom." I filled her in on some of the details.

"Sounds really hot. You really like her, Jean." She could see it by the enthusiasm in my eyes.

"I'm crazy about her. She's smart, sensitive, and a great conversationalist."

Rachel quickly changed the mood. "Heard anything from Martha?" She was our mutual friend.

"Nope. She needs some time to get used to the separation. I'll call her in a couple of weeks."

"Does she know about Robin?"

"Nope."

"Who else have you told?"

"Nobody. You're my best friend."

"Take it slow, Jean." She seemed worried. "What about her boyfriend?"

"Oh, him. I always forget about him. She acts as if he is not alive."

"That's strange." Rachel stopped. "Be careful, Jean. You make yourself too vulnerable."

"I'll be fine. I just have to pass this freaking exam, and then I can sort it all out. I won't do anything else until then."

"Good."

"How's Morris?" I reverted to my Jewish grandmother accent.

"Great. He's such a nice guy. He makes me feel so warm inside."

I always start to get bored at this point in the conversation.

"He brought over champagne last night and I dressed up for him in a new red teddy. He loved it."

"Do you ever hear from Penny anymore?" I changed the subject to her previous affair.

"She's getting married next month. She's met a really nice guy." Penny and Rachel had dated for close to a year before Penny decided that she needed to get out of the relationship because she had fallen out of love with Rachel. Rachel was devastated. I think that's when she gave up girls altogether.

"I guess, if one really had a choice, it would be easier being straight. It seems fashionable right now for gay women to meet guys. Must be part of the backlash Susan Faludi writes about. Instead of buying more *Cosmopolitans* and being hoodwinked into thinking women have to smell, look, and feel like the women in the pictures, we think that we have to be straight. There is just no future in being a lesbian."

"Come on, Jean, don't be so cynical. If I were gay, I'd be with a woman, but I'm BI and I'm really in love with Morris." Rachel seemed sincere.

"I guess you must be." I usually don't believe things that BI women say. If they were really honest with themselves, wouldn't they be gay? I'm honest and I'm gay. Right!

Pizzas finished, I told Rachel more about Robin: the thought of her made my underwear wet; I just couldn't get her out of my mind. I'd never met anybody like her before. How I wanted to run off with her to Italy and spend the year cultivating my father's garden in the hills of Tuscany while I wrote my dissertation and she did the dishes. I'm kidding, not the dishes! I'd find something else for her to do.

Rachel brought me back to reality. "Why are you doing this to yourself?" she asked.

"What do you mean? Doesn't this Italy thing sound romantic?"

I quickly responded.

"You are headed for trouble. She has a boyfriend."

"I can handle it," I said with conviction.

"Maybe you should try and work things out with Martha."
"I can't. She's in Boston. I'm totally over her. I can't even touch her." I felt guilty saying it. "Rachel," I started coming down from my euphoric state; like a crack in the drapes, I let a little reality shine through. "I can't live alone right now. I am fragile and out of control."

Rachel put her hand on my shoulder and said, "You need to be kinder to yourself."

Being loving seemed impossible. I had to crash. That was my way. Feel the most excruciating of love pains. After that I would have no alternative. I would have to confront things, become a better person. I knew that Robin was the end and the beginning. I needed to touch rock bottom, push off with both legs, and float back to the surface of my life. This is my attempt at being a kinder and more compassionate person. Try getting Rachel or anyone to understand that.

Rachel tried to comfort me, but after just a brief respite, a glimpse of reality, a few tears in my eyes, the drapes shut again and I was in the darkness of a small room surrounded by my parents' angry words.

"When will I see you again, Rachel?" I asked as we walked home.

"I'll meet you first thing after you finish it. We'll celebrate."

"I just hope there is reason to celebrate." I wasn't convinced I'd actually pass the damn thing.

"You worry about everything. I'll talk to you later in the week."

We hugged each other in the customary way, and I was alone again with my twisted thoughts of Robin, the Fatal Attraction lover or the girl of my dreams. Which was the truth?

A couple of homeless men asked me for money on the corner of 116th Street and Broadway. As usual, I looked them straight in the face and told them that I was sorry but that I didn't have any, which was really a lie since I had a pocket full of change. For about half a block, I felt guilty for not having given them any money. My thoughts quickly drifted to Robin, and how I missed her. Did she remember me? It was a week since I had last seen her. Maybe it was all over.

The answering machine was blinking at me when I entered my room. The first message was from my mother, who reminded me that she and Dad were coming home and to pick them up at the airport. As if I didn't remember. The second was from Monica, who had some info for my exam, and the third was a hang-up. I felt sick. Robin did not call. So what if I had asked her not to call? She would have called me anyway if she was madly in love with me.

I walked to the garage on 125th Street to get our gray Volvo. Mamma and Dad were arriving at Kennedy Airport in an hour. I hadn't thought much about them all summer. Now the thought of having to deal with them started to weigh heavy on my mind. The first thing my Mamma would say was that my hair was too long and bushy, the second was that I had put on a couple of pounds, and third was, "Gosh, how could you spend the whole summer in New York? It's so damn hot." At least Mamma tried to carry on a conversation. Dad sat and stewed in the back of the car wondering why Mamma has to take tons of luggage from Italy to the U.S. Olive oil, gas lamps, place mats, and vinegar were usually schlepped from Italy to America.

The weather was typically clear for early September. Dad had to get back for a week to finalize a book contract. Otherwise they would have just as well stayed in Italy. As they get older, they have less and less tolerance for New York's inconveniences; they'd be better off retiring to Tuscany, Italy's Marin County.

125th Street was jammed with double- and triple-parked cars. Rap music thumped as I waited at the light. A large woman with two children smiled as she passed me. Her child busily licked an ice cream while it melted onto her clothes. I wonder if my mother ever let me enjoy an ice cream like that. She would have ripped it out of my hands and slapped my behind and said I was a slob like my father. A gypsy cab cut me off when the light turned green. I did not give him the finger or any other hand gesture. Dad gave a guy the finger once when he was cut off, and the guy spent the next ten minutes trying to sideswipe Dad and me off of the Whitestone Bridge. Instead of reacting to rude drivers, I now use the same energy to cut other people off and not feel bad about it.

I stared straight in front of me until some impatient driver blasted the horn. I raced to the toll clerk at the Triboro Bridge to make up for lost time. She ripped the money out of my hand as I said thank you. Shouldn't she be thanking me? I've never quite understood New York tollbooth etiquette.

I love going to the airport. Each summer, since I was a one-year-old, Mamma packed up Dad and the kids for two months of vacation in the Italian Alps, while all my friends went to some silly, mosquito-infested camp upstate. As a kid, I had an entire ritual of air travel. I carried a knapsack filled with three books, cards, a Walkman (post 1975 or whenever), some stationary, a toothbrush, tampons (I just never knew with my period), a picture of one of my friends with whom I was in love, and my passport.

The D'Entreves family arrived at least three hours prior to departure to get the best selection of seats. We sat in different parts of the plane. Brother sat in the smoking section, near the sexy girls who drank gin and tonics the whole flight. Dad usually chose an aisle seat in the middle of the plane because it was far enough away from Mamma. Mamma and I sat together. She wanted a window seat so that she could watch the wings shift and make sure that everything was in proper running order. I sat next to her because I thought our family should sit together like the other families on the plane.

I parked the car in the British Airways parking lot, in the area farthest away from the terminal, the way Dad liked it. This way he would know that I did not spend any extraneous time looking for a closer spot but, rather, just sped straight to the farthest spot and walked a couple of extra yards to the terminal. He would be impressed while bitching about Mamma's heavy baggage.

I was fifteen minutes early, so I decided to grab a quick beer at the airport bar. The waitress from Queens brought me a Coors Light, some flight peanuts, and a four-dollar check. This guy to my right was eyeing a woman sitting at the bar. She was particularly attractive, and I wished that I could go up to her and buy her a drink. I suppose I couldn't for two reasons: she may not be gay and she may just want to be alone. Anyway, she looked just slightly on the seedy side. Long brown hair, turquoise jewelry, and jeans—bet she was a drug trafficker or an undercover cop. I was entertaining myself.

The muffled voice, with a distinguished Queens / Puerto Rican accent, announced that flight BA 125 from Pisa and London had just landed. I savored the last drops of the beer, gave a quick glance at the Cher look-alike at the bar, felt a good buzz, and walked over to the gate. A frantic teenager who forgot his passport ran over to a phone. Old women limped around, waiting uncomfortably for a flight. Passing time in airports is like eating Chinese food; after a couple of hours, you forget that you ever did it.

I gently shoved a young lady with a big balloon saying "I love you" and a kid on her arm so that I could get a spot along the rail to see my folks come out of customs. The kid was very bored and spent the next five minutes trying to hit me with his balloon. This other short guy next to me inched a little too close. Finding space as a single woman is so difficult at times.

Mamma was the first one out. My heart raced with happiness. She spotted me right away. Dad crawled behind with the luggage. I ran over and gave her a bear hug and a kiss.

She looked me up and down and said, "You losta some weight. You looka good." I felt relieved pleasing her.

"But when are you agoing to cutta yoo hair? Nexta time you come to Italy, I'll take you to mya favorite lady, Marisa, in Florence. She doesa such a good job." She pointed to her color, trim, and set job.

"Don't you like it?"

"Yes Mamma." She had beige hair. Dad looked tired and unhappy.

"It's good to see you," he said.

I kissed his cheek and grabbed one of the bags.

We made our way through the dense crowd of travelers, cabbies, and family members.

"Dad, wait here. I'll run and get the car. I parked it pretty far because there were no spots." He was impressed.

"I don't mind the walk. Ma, you stay here a second, and we'll go get the car." Another golden opportunity to get away from Mamma.

"When's the big day?" He put a meek arm around me.

"Day after tomorrow. Dad, I'm so worried. I've practically stopped eating."

"You'll do fine. For the next two days you should go to the

movies. That's what I did before my orals."

"But Dad, I...."

"Jean, you've been studying all summer. You'll do fine."

"I guess, but Sally and Robert from school are in the library twelve hours a day. They are there now."

We got to the gray Volvo, and Dad gave it a cursory examination for any summertime damage I might have caused it. Satisfied that I hadn't gotten into any accidents, he jumped into the passenger seat and asked if I had put any oil in the engine lately.

"You know this car uses a lot of oil."

"I checked it last week."

We drove up to where Mamma was standing, with a face as if she was entertaining the thought that we were never going to return to retrieve her. She hopped into the back seat and made a grunting sound.

"It's so hotta here." She always said that when she came back from the Alps. "Thank God a for that cool mountain air. Are a you ever going to come to my Italy again?" she asked me. This was her way of telling me that she missed me this summer. This way she filled me with guilt. "I thinka you coulda have taken at leasta two weeks off to see yoo mother." I did not feel like responding to this prodding.

"So how's Davide, Mona, and the kids?" I asked, regarding my uncle, aunt, and cousins.

"They are depressed and taking Librax. Your cousin Violetta has a boyfriend. They may be married next year." Dad filled me in.

"Great." I started to feel sick.

We were back to the straight lifestyle again.

"How'sa Martha?" Mamma asked politely.

"We broke up last week," I told her coldly. I knew that she

liked Martha because Martha took care of me and genuinely loved me.

"Did you finda somebody else?" She knew my patterns well enough.

"No, I just need to be alone for a while. You know, the exam and everything."

"Isa she angry with you?"

"Yes, she doesn't want to speak to me for a while."

"Poora thing, she isa such a nice girl." A wave of sickness gripped my stomach. It felt like death.

"Dad, how's your book coming?" Dad was busy writing a book on contemporary Italian culture.

"I'd like you to read a chapter or two to see what you think. Do you think you'll have any time?"

"Give me a couple of weeks to pass this exam and recover, then I'll be happy to see it."

Dad always got very interested in a discussion when it had to do with his work. Funny how that was.

"I'm writing about the effects of anorexia nervosa on Italian literature." He is tackling an issue about women! All the information he dug up in the archives in Florence on Leon Battista Alberti must have dried up for him to do anything about women. He told me when I was growing up that one should study only the great works of the masters, not the tinkerings of second-rate women.

"What's the theme of your book?"

"What do you mean by theme?" he asked impatiently. "I already told you what it was about."

"What are you trying to argue?"

He started to get nervous. Did he not already explain it to me? "It's about eating disorders and art."

"I see, Dad." I was safer talking about the Yankees.

"How'sa yoo brother?" Mamma asked. The family never referred to each other by their first names. It was always sister, mother, Mamma, Dad. Mom got our names mixed up anyway, often beginning conversations with Fred, Pappa, Mamma, and finally landing on Jean like a roulette ball on a number. It kept a certain distance between us, not that it wasn't there already. I think that's why I got into this terrible habit two or three months into a comfortable relationship with a woman of calling her some stupid nickname like sweety, honey, puppy, bunny (ugh), or lovey. I needed the same kind of distance.

We came to a stop on the corner of 125th Street and Second Avenue. An old black man with a white beard bent down and asked me if I wanted the windshield cleaned for a quarter. My mother got very nervous and told me to roll up the window and turn on the windshield wipers. Dad sat up straight. I told the guy that my windows were clean and that I didn't need a wipe. He moved on the to Mercedes behind me.

"It's really the end of the world," Dad said.

"Is it really any worse than some old, congested neighborhood in Rome?" I asked, never having been there.

"Noooo," my mother asserted loudly. "Rome maya be a mess, but it hasa tradition."

"Oh." What bullshit. So does Harlem. Harlem was black and that was the main problem. My mother was openly racist—she did not seem to know it.

We finally reached the haven of Morningside Heights and the Columbia neighborhood. You could see the tense expressions ease on their faces as we drove up the steep hill dividing Harlem from the Upper West Side.

"Well, this isa certainly a littlea better," my mother announced, explaining, "Ata leasta there are somea trees."

My mother had a long, checkered past with 125th Street. For

some reason, on two different occasions when she was driving on that street, the car stopped dead, and she had to get out and call the family to get a tow-truck. I'll never forget one of those times, when I went to retrieve her in a cab and found her in the car locked up tight, windows shut, on a 90-degree late spring day.

My summer vacation officially over, I dropped my parents off and drove the car back to the garage.

Chapter 5

I awoke at 6:15 the morning of my exam and went for a walk in Riverside Park. It was a gray day. Rain dripped off trees when the wind blew lazily. At the clearing at 104th Street, where Puerto Rican guys play chess, I looked up at the sky and asked for support from the forces in heaven. I was ready. If I could play piano on WNYC radio when I was ten, I could do this. If I could sink two clutch free throws at the end of regulation, I could do this. If I could survive the cold wind of the parental return, I could do this. But in reality, I was never good at any of these things.

I asked for Miriam's support. She is my friend the spiritual healer, who can heal the whole world with the wave of a hand and tell you your future for the next two weeks in intimate detail, but cannot admit to herself that she is a dyke. My father introduced her to me one day in Italy. She works as the accountant at the Villa I Tatti, a fashionable enclave for Renaissance scholars in Florence. As a young woman growing up in Florence with a Swedish father and Italian mother, she wanted to pursue a career in psychology. After attending numerous lectures at the university, she came to realize that psychology did not make any sense. She then left Florence for several years and traveled to Arizona, where she worked with American Indian healers. She learned the fine art of energy transferal and retrieval, and when she returned to Italy, she set up an informal practice with some of her friends. In the meantime, she found herself a practical job that ensured her a weekly paycheck, for she never accepted any money for her spiritual services. Not kosher.

I met her two summers ago in Tuscany. (You can read more about her in *Fiammetta*.) She bought a house in the country about two miles away from where my parents owned a small villa. The day we met she drove me to Vinci, the birthplace of Leonardo the painter. She told me that she wanted me to experience a special place. In her Fiat 500, we rumbled up the rugged countryside, lined with tortured olive trees.

"I come here when I'm feeling depressed." She raced through the ancient metal gate and parked the car on the edge of the driveway.

The ground was hot and orange as we walked over to the special place.

"See?" she said triumphantly, as if she had just opened a box with all her jewelry in it.

I felt somewhat puzzled as I looked up to see a huge old oak tree, with an assortment of Tuscan lovers embraced under it. Miriam led me to the trunk of the tree and told me to look inside the ancient knob. Big green and blue flies buzzed around the tree's open sore, and I winced with surprise.

"Do you feel anything?" Miriam looked at me earnestly.

"Like what?" I was confused.

"Do you feel the spirit of Leonardo? He came to sit under this tree when he was young."

"Oh." I tried hard to feel something. Suddenly from out of the blue, literally, an enormous gust of wind shook the old branches. We looked at each other.

"That is his spirit, Jean. He has introduced himself to you."

I looked up at the deep green leaves in amazement. "You mean he is still here?"

"All you have to do is think of him, and he will appear to you in a feeling." She rubbed her palms on the rough bark and smiled as if possessed. "Now he will be forever a part of you."

For someone who was raised without any religion, this was an extremely spiritual moment for me. I felt something beyond my mundane life. I knew there was a force greater than that of my silly existence. Miriam hugged me, and we walked over to the high brick wall that looked out over the olive groves.

"Can everyone feel his power?" I was hoping he could help my lost mother.

"You just have to be willing to let go and experience the other world."

Back on Riverside Drive, I had summoned Miriam's spirit and she had answered me in the customary way: an enormous gust of wind—from out of nowhere—swept through the trees. She was with me. Everything would be just fine.

Back home, I put on all my luckiest clothes: the pink T-shirt with an insignia from a gay resort, my green sweat-shirt, my pink-checkered mountain-climbing pants, two pairs of sweat socks, and Nike sneakers. I grabbed three pens, two pencils, and French, English, and Latin dictionaries. Mamma said "in bocca'l lupo" and Dad repeated not to worry about it.

If I passed this one, I really will have pulled the wool over their eyes at Columbia. They'd promote an imbecile. More likely I wouldn't pass, and they would finally be able to see that I was really too stupid to get a Ph.D.

No one is around the campus at 7:45 a.m., except for an occasional aerobics enthusiast or grouchy guard. I jumped up the steps to the music office and waited for Professor Morris. This was my last chance to bail out before the biggest defeat of my life. The terror of the day overtook my body, and I contemplated going back out of the building and jumping into the subway for Pennsylvania Station and on to anywhere in the country.

I heard the elevator door open. A chipper professor came skipping out with keys in his hand.

"I'll be just a moment. Have you had anything to eat?" he asked kindly.

"Yes." I waited nervously for him to gather the blue books and the exam. He walked me upstairs and opened the door to an empty classroom.

"As you know, you have eight hours to complete the exam. I encourage you, however, to take an hour for lunch. If you have any questions, I'll be downstairs in my office. See you at four." And he was gone.

My fate was dispersed over six pieces of paper. The first piece contained a choice of essay questions, and the other five were Xerox copies of ancient documents in three different languages. I started writing at 8:15 and didn't pick my head off the paper until 1:30. Four questions answered, I knew in my heart that I would pass. One was on Machaut and Landini—stuff I knew cold.

All the studying had paid off, and the fear of failure disappeared. All I had to do was finish the damn thing and I would succeed. I could see my beloved Robin again. I could drink lots of beer again. I told myself that I needed a break and left the room to get a hot dog from the vendor on the corner of 116th Street and Broadway. It was my tradition to eat a hot dog in the midst of a life-defining endeavor. The afternoon that I aced the master's exam, I got a hot dog. The afternoon of my big basketball game against those goons from Brown University, I got a hot dog.

The sky had brightened, and it felt good to be out of that cramped room.

"Two with mustard and a Coke, please," I ordered.

He looked at me up and down, as was customary for guys

who sell hot dogs on the street, and asked me what my major was.

"Music," I said with a smile.

"Wandaful! My sister plays the piano."

"Great," I lied.

"Four dollars," he said, handing me the goods and getting a straw.

By the time I reached the music building, I had wolfed down the dogs and drunk most of the soda. As you know, I practically stopped eating three weeks before the exam because I thought I should be punished like a nun lobbying for sainthood in medieval Italy.

On my way back to the exam cell, I said hello to Bob the nosy librarian and Sally the repressed Bach professor. They wished me luck and looked twice at my special, lucky outfit. I sat down at the desk and began to answer the second-to-last question on English fourteenth-century songs. Who really cares about this stuff anyway? What was the point? Tired cynicism was entering my brain. Halfway through, I put my pen down and placed my fat head on the desk. I started dreaming of Robin's smooth skin, which I hadn't seen or touched for two weeks.

"Oh shit, I'm losing it." I wanted to take a nap. Suddenly I heard a thunderous crash. The window had blown open and smashed into the wall. I looked up to see the window snap shut again. Temporarily rattled, I held my breath for ten seconds and let out a sigh. It was Miriam, I thought, telling me that things were going to go fine. She was giving me one last sign of encouragement.

The final two and a half hours of the exam passed by quickly, with only an occasional cramp in my right wrist. Folding up the exam into a neat pile with the blue books, I picked up the stack of dictionaries, opened the door, gave the room one last indecent gesture, and stumbled happily down to the professor's office.

"It's done, Professor Morris. Now it's all yours."

"How do you feel?"

"As if I need to sleep for two weeks straight."

"Your results will be ready in three days. I'll call you as soon as we have made an evaluation."

"Thanks again for everything, Professor." I still felt like I owed him something.

I ran out the building door and skipped all the way home. Miriam had communicated to me that I had passed, the questions were fair, and I could go back to my relationship with Robin-the new love of my life.

On the table in the lobby of my apartment, I found two sets of flowers intended for me. The first was from Martha and had been professionally delivered by some flower firm. The card read, "Good luck, I know you'll pass." The second was of the Korean market variety, hand-delivered by some secret admirer. The card read, "Thinking of you and wishing you the best results, Robin." I was ecstatic. My two favorite people in the world had remembered the exam and me.

I jumped into the elevator, did a little jig, and got off on the fifth floor. Mamma and Dad weren't home, thank God. I could have the whole apartment to myself and blast the stereo with my favorite Madonna song, "Justify My Love," while looking at my bare shoulders in the mirror and posing in various muscle-head stances. After working up a sweat, I ran to the phone and called my beloved, Robin.

"Hey, Robin."

Her voice started to smile. "Heeeyy. How did it go?"

"I think I passed, I think I passed." I convinced myself. It didn't sound possible. "When can I see you? I am dying to hold you again."

She hesitated. "I've got a lot of work to finish before I can go home." My heart sank. "Come by tonight after ten. If there is a problem, I'll call you first."

How could I ever wait five hours to see her? This was torture. Romeo would have flipped out if he had had to wait for Juliet to finish a project.

"I'll see you later."

I called Rachel in a panic. "Thank God you're home."

"How did the exam go?"

"Fine. I'm pretty sure I passed. Unless there is someone on the committee who doesn't like dykes, it's smooth sailing."

"Great! Congratulations."

"Robin can't see me until ten."

"So?"

"Ten." I repeated. "I can't wait that long.

"Jean, calm down. She's got a different kind of job than you do. She's on deadline, big clients, powerful partners."

"What about love? Fuck work."

"Let's go get a slice of pizza."

"I'm still nauseated from sitting through that exam. I'm not hungry."

"Just sit with me then."

"See you in ten minutes in front of the Chock-Full-of-Nuts."

"OK." I slammed down the phone, pumped up Madonna, and danced in the mirror.

Rachel was dressed in an old T-shirt she probably slept in the night before. She hugged me and said that I looked good but tired.

"You need to get some sleep, Jean. You're burned out."

"I want to see Robin tonight. Every hour without her is torture."

"I haven't seen you so excited about anyone since Debbie Barnard five years ago. And you remember what happened with her."

"She didn't tell me that she was doing my basketball coach right before doing me. That was the last time I felt suicidal."

We had our usual slice and a soda at Happy Pizza. Rachel talked about Morris while I talked about Robin. We didn't talk to each other. It was as if we were each drinking: getting high on what we were saying, while being completely oblivious to the world around us. I looked at my watch abruptly.

"Only four more hours until I see my love. I think I'll survive."

Rachel walked me home, and I went to sleep until the alarm awakened me to the darkness of the night. For a panicked split second, I thought I had missed my date with Robin.

After another session of lesbian primping and a murky subway ride, I made my way to Robin's East Side apartment. The Hispanic doorman asked me my name.

"Jean," I replied. Sometimes I like to say Marilyn to see what kind of a reaction I get. That's such a sexy, loaded name. It's hard for a tough dyke to wear well.

"What?" he asked. Doormen never get your name right the first time. I think thatthey just want to look at you for a longer period of time before you bolt for the elevators—then they focus on your butt. It's a power thing.

"Jean." I said it slower: "J--e--a--nnnnn."

"Hello, yes, Jean is here," he said into the telephone. He paused. "Go right up."

"Thank you." Whatever.

Because I was so wasted the last time I was here, I had forgotten what the building and Robin's apartment looked like. It made this trip all the more exciting for me. I could discover everything again.

She was waiting for me with one hand on the doorknob and the other holding a phone to her ear. She mouthed that her mother was on the phone and showed me over to the sofa, where there were two glasses of red wine already poured on the coffee table.

"I saw the convention. Did you like Kennedy? I thought he was goofy. The two people with HIV? No, I missed them. Christopher Reeve is incredible, isn't he? Poor family. Grandma, no I haven't heard a word from her. I'm going up to visit in two weeks. I wish you could come too. It's been so rainy here. No, I'm fine, you don't have to. I have a jacket. OK, tell Dad hello, I'll speak to you during the week. Yeah, Yeah. Bye, Bye." She hung up the phone and let out a grand sigh as if she was hiding something.

"So how do you feel?" She sat down on the chair in front of me. Everything was very proper.

"Great—come here." I motioned.

"No, I'm fine where I am. Phil wanted me to go down this weekend. And I told him I had to work," she said with some guilt.

"I see." I didn't because I was delirious to be with her. "You're going to spend the weekend with me. Sounds like more fun."

I was kidding but at the same time looking to see if she agreed in her face or eyes. I continued, "I have something for you."

"What?" She seemed to be more at ease.

"I made you a copy of Hildegard of Bingen's greatest hits. She's the bomb in medieval music.

I skipped over to her tape deck and popped in the selection.

"Her music puts me in touch with the higher powers." Suddenly I remembered Hilde wasn't Jewish and made three apologies about all her references to the Virgin Mary, which

Robin wouldn't understand anyway since she did not take Latin in high school.

Strains of Hildegard's sequence to Saint Maximinus streamed into the Manhattan apartment. A drone instrument grumbled beneath the undulating melodic line.

"This is beautiful, Jean," she said in a reserved tone.

"Let's sit quietly for a few minutes and let it touch our souls." How corny. But you should really forgive me, I'm in love.

Not particularly convinced by my spirituality, Robin closed her eyes as I stared at her absolutely beautiful person. I must be in heaven. My favorite person in the world accompanied by musical angels.

After the first selection, Robin got up and went to the bathroom.

"Would you like something to eat?" She asked from behind the bathroom door.

"No, I'm fine. Hurry back." She was dressed in a tight-fitting, dark blue bodysuit and pale blue jeans. Her dark, wavy hair followed her as she walked back toward me. This time she sat next to me.

"Jean, I've missed you so much these last two weeks."

"Me too, but now it's over. We can spend our free time together."

"I . . . ."

"Yes?"

"I have a lot of work to do: two new clients and a huge project to complete. I'm just not sure how much time we really have."

"We'll make the time." I comforted her. I raised her head and kissed her gently on her full lips. She kissed me back and inserted her tongue into my mouth.

I began to moan slightly with delight. "Have you any idea how beautiful you are?" I asked her.

She smiled and led me to her bedroom, where we made love for the next four hours. Sheets and pillows flew with fervor as we experimented with every position imaginable. I stopped counting the number of orgasms after three. She begged me for more, and I grabbed her by the back of her hair, slammed her head to the pillow, and plunged my tongue into her mouth. After she came for the third time, I held her in my arms and massaged her back. After several minutes, she fell asleep, and I dozed off ten minutes later while listening to her contented snores.

The telephone woke us from our state of bliss. She let it ring twice and then jumped out of bed before the answering machine picked up.

"Yes, what time is it? So late? I overslept. I miss you too. What? No, I stayed in last night. I was so exhausted from this week. Next week? Maybe. Maybe I'll come down. It's not such a good idea for you to come right now. I've got no time."

I started to wake up around this point in the conversation. She was speaking in a very hushed tone, but nothing low enough that a well-trained musicologist couldn't pick up.

"Yeah, how's the cat? Still sick? I talked to mother last night. She said you came by the other night for dinner. Same old stuff. Listen, Phil, can I call you back later today? I've got to get ready for work. I'll speak to you from the office, OK. . . . Me too. Bye."

"How's Phil?" I asked with a lump of reality in my throat.

"He's fine." She jumped on top of me and kissed by neck. "I missed you when I was out of bed. Kiss me."

Though I was feeling slightly nauseated from Phil's phone call, she didn't seem to remember him at all and made passionate love to me for the next two hours or so.

The day was glorious and Robin never left my side.

We said mushy things to each other because we were in love. In Central Park, a man and woman rolled by us on their colorful blades.

"God, I hate that," I declared. (It was still my crabby phase in life.)

"Did you ever try? It's really fun." She defended the relatively new urban pastime.

"No, that's not what I mean. It bothers me the way guys and their girlfriends interact during the activity. She holds on to him for dear life. He drags her down the path. I think it's a good metaphor for the way women are educated to do things in this culture. When boys learn to skate, they go solo, crash, get up, get bruised, skate, and after a while, learn how to do it right. When young women learn, they ask their boyfriends to teach them and then proceed to hold on to them the whole time so that they never learn to do it right—or alone. They can't develop self-esteem that way. Not to mention any flair."

Robin listened quietly. Usually she defended the foibles of straight people from my comments, but in this instance she couldn't find anything to defend.

"I think you're right. It happens in architecture school too. How many times did I hear young female students run up to the guys and ask them sheepishly for help with a model? They'd learn more if they finished it on their own."

Having agreed on that last detail of my feminist philosophy, we sat down on a park bench facing the river and ate our bagels with cream cheese and lox. She leaned against my shoulder.

"What was it like growing up in Italy?" she asked me.

"The greatest. I've only experienced those feelings of joy twice again in my life. Being with you is one; the other was my last day as an inventory manager at Alfa Romeo, when I wrote a resignation letter to my boss that ended with 'so fuck you.' I never sent it."

"Come on, Jean. Tell me what it was like."

"I spent my summers climbing the Italian Alps. Then when Dad was on sabbatical, I went to first and seventh grades at the American School of Florence. Those were the best years of my stupid life."

"Why stupid?"

"I don't know. I've always felt that artists should struggle and contemplate about how stupid their lives are."

"So?" she prodded.

"My school was in a medieval castle that hung above Florence. It housed all twelve grades. We studied math, English, Italian, and art history. Recess was spent chasing butterflies in the manicured gardens in the maze of tall green hedges. I remember being the only female member of the chess team. We went to Rome to play the American School of Rome. I think we got killed. Robin, this is difficult for me to talk about. I rarely do."

"Why? It sounds so beautiful."

"It's because I have never been able to get rid of the pain I suffered when I came back to New Rochelle High School. No one talked to me anymore. Old friends pretended I wasn't alive, or that I was a weird new kid from Manhattan. I became a recluse. I realized that I might be a lesbian. I was miserable."

"I'm sorry to hear that, Jean." She held me tighter.

Anyway, let me try to remember Florence. . . . I loved every minute I was alive. We had a soccer team that played on the *piazza* in front of the castle. I was so excited to play that I wouldn't sleep for days before the games. I'd just look out the window of my home with my dog, Bobbie, and dream of scoring. Bobbie was a temperamental Tuscan mutt that Dad promised me we would get when we left New Rochelle for a year in Italy. He growled at my Italian piano teacher every time she came to give me a lesson. He barked at my friend Kara, who smoked cigarettes all the time. He stayed with me for most of the day. Am I boring you yet?"

"No, your voice is so soothing."

I put down the rest of my bagel, wiped my fingers, and caressed the inside of her thigh.

"You are kind to listen to me. I've really never told these stories to anyone. I felt so lonely as a child. Bobbie was my closet companion. Every afternoon we took long walks up the sides of the hills of Fiesole, where my folks had rented a house. The roads were hot and rocky, and ancient walls were covered with spiny blackberry bushes. One day while investigating my neighbor's property, we found a mysterious place: an old, humid grotto. It was tucked away under some rambling vines. A postcard of the Virgin Mary was tacked up on the furthest wall. Two benches faced one another and between them was a slab of rock, where I played solitaire."

Robin smiled at me. "Why were you so lonely as a child?"

"I'm not exactly sure. I saw myself as a suffocated, misunderstood weirdo, whose object in life was to struggle."

"That sounds ridiculous. Didn't your parents see how sad you were?"

"They never seemed particularly concerned. Dad really was rarely around. Too busy in the Florentine archives. Mamma was usually in a bad mood. She spent most of the day swatting the dog off the couch with her broom."

"You were neglected."

"No, not at all. My mother paid attention to me all day. She never left me alone. Always criticizing what I wore, how I walked, the music I played. Let's not talk about the difficult stuff. Plus, I'm tired of talking about myself."

I placed the remainders of both of our bagels into the paper bag. "You want any more orange juice?"

"No thanks." She put her head on my lap. I couldn't believe the joy I felt. I rubbed the back of her soft neck with my hand while watching a stinky tugboat drift by.

"That feels great. I could just doze off again."

"Go ahead. I'm enjoying you."

"Jean?" Her voice sounded more serious.

"Yes?"

"Will you promise me something?"

"What?"

"Will you promise to always be my friend?"

"Why do you ask that?"

"Because I care so much about you. I just never want to lose you in my life."

"Why would that ever happen?"

"I don't know. I can't lose you the way I did my sister."

"My darling Robin. I promise that I will always be there for you." I bent down and kissed her lips. I held her until my arms started to throb, and then I held her a little more.

Robin glanced down at her watch. It was 3:15. She said she wanted to go home.

"Let's take showers and maybe catch a movie," I suggested.

"OK, but I have to call Phil back. He's waiting."

"What does he want?" I asked. My heart was in my throat.

"He wanted to come down this weekend, but I told him that I had to work."

"So?"

"I need to call him to tell him everything is OK."

"You have to check in with him every day?"

"What's wrong with that? Wouldn't you want to know where I am everyday?"

"I guess."

We got to her apartment, and I told her that she should go call Phil and that I would meet her in an hour. She seemed relieved that she didn't have to suggest the alternative herself. I walked up the block as if there was no problem. RIGHT.

My first stop was the corner bookstore. I went through the two rows of women's studies books, then made my way to the biographies, then to the trashy novels. I picked up an old book by Jacqueline Suzanne, whose cover had a picture of a large-breasted seventies-type woman. This looks about my speed right now, I thought. Next I walked across Second Avenue to a bar that had pictures of Lech Walesa on its window. I sat down, ordered a pint of Bass, and began to get bombed.

I pulled out my Jacqueline Suzanne novel and thumbed to the pages with the sex. She was really good at that stuff. The bartender asked me if I wanted another one, and I just told him to keep them coming.

"Can I get you something to eat, Miss?" He must have seen the distress in my face.

"No, I'm fine. All I want is beer."

In the bar's afternoon light, I started reading my new novel. Jeff, the handsome real estate tycoon, was busy making love to the lonely, desperate wife of a banker, who had never really made love until this night with Jeff. I never believed a word of that stuff because deep down inside I never believed that a man could possibly know how to make love to a woman. Lesbians who have been with men before say there is just no comparison. Women are the greatest—we are more sensitive, caring, and affectionate. I believed all this stuff, and I was going to show Robin that I could be much better than Phil. My thoughts were beginning to get drunk.

"I'll have another one, please."

I read over the same paragraph several times. When you are

drunk and upset, it is difficult to absorb anything, let alone literature. Jeff was so sexy, the way he fondled her breasts and sucked on her belly.

My fourth beer came to an end. I walked over to the pay phone near the toilet to call Robin. I didn't want to return while she was still on the phone.

"Jean, where are you?" she asked me in an edgy voice.

"I went to the bookstore and stopped for a beer."

"Come home fast."

"I'll be there in ten minutes." I felt good because she missed me.

I set twenty dollars on the bar and waved good-bye to the bartender. He must have thought I was such a loser: no boyfriend, no make-up, and no future.

Robin was waiting for me at the door as I walked out of the elevator. I had a six-pack of Coors Light in my hands.

"I thought I'd pick us up something to drink."

She grabbed the package from my hand and led me into the bedroom.

"I missed you so much, Jean. Thanks for letting me talk to Phil. Thanks for being so considerate."

"No problem," I slurred.

She kissed me hard on the lips and stroked my right hand.

"He's staying home with his folks this weekend. They are old and appreciate it when he can do some of the yard work for them."

"I see. So, when are you going to tell him?" Suddenly the mood changed.

"Eventually. I don't think that he could handle it right now."

"Why not?"

"I don't know. He was planning to move up here in December, sell his condo and everything."

"What?" I said in disbelief. I got up and crossed the room.

"Don't worry, he is not coming anytime soon. I told him I needed more time to think about that kind of heavy commitment."

I was confused. "Why didn't you tell me about this?"

"I thought that it never was going to happen. I don't want him here. I want to be with you."

"I can't just keep living as if Phil doesn't exist. What are your future plans? Are you planning to get married? Come on, Robin. What the hell is going on here?"

She was frightened. I had never become angry with her before.

"Please don't yell at me—I can't take it." Tears began to swell in her eyes.

"Don't you understand? I love you. I would do anything for you."

"How do you know?" She suddenly sounded cold.

"I've never met anybody like you. You're wonderful, alive, interesting. I just really, really like you."

"Why?" She was very serious.

"What do you mean, why? Why do I have to explain? I love you." I crossed over to the bed and hugged her hard. "I love you. Can't you see?"

"Those are just empty words."

I had never had to deal with something so frustrating before. How do you explain to someone what love is? It was especially hard for me since I, too, was clueless about the word's meaning. Everybody knows what it is. It's like the sun or the moon or the rain. You just feel it. It's very Italian, all-encompassing. Debilitating.

Like a wrong turn on the highway right before getting to a destination, our love affair had suddenly careened off track.

She must not love me. My heart sank.

"Do you love me? I asked her.

"I can't tell you since I don't know what love is. Please, back off. Now you're starting to sound like Phil."

Robin would be a project—probably the most difficult one I'd have to face. Certainly there was Wendy the bulimic, or Nancy the alcoholic, or Martha afraid of intimacy. Robin didn't know what love was. Wow. I was ready for the challenge. I wanted to save her. I wanted to show her how to love. I would show her how to love like Francesca and Paolo, Romeo and Juliet, Tony and Maria, Alice and Gertrude. As if I knew.

"Have you ever been in love before?" I started class from the beginning.

"Phil and I began seeing each other just before I started architecture school. He was a couple of years younger than I was. I think I was in love with him then.

"That doesn't sound very convincing. Any other time?"

She had come completely unglued by this point and answered angrily.

"I don't need you to patronize me."

Tears suddenly began to swell in my eyes. Robin's coldness was tearing me apart. I stared at her in disbelief. Who is this person?

We spent the next three weeks in uninterrupted bliss. I pretended that Phil was not alive, and she pretended that she was in love with me. We slept with each other every night. We held each other tightly and let go only to go to the bathroom. I bought her a small gift every day. She said thank you, but gave me nothing in return. She stopped telling me when Phil called, what he said, and what she said back. One day, while lecturing on the final scene of Verdi's opera *Aida*, I told my class that I could relate to why Aida snuck into the tomb with Radames, where she would suffocate with her beloved. Because, like me, she was madly in love. The class seemed bewildered by my personal admission, but I truly was the starry-eyed heroine. Love could never defeat me. Robin was ecstatic, clearly mad about me, and though I never asked her again how she felt, I knew it.

She invited me to her architecture functions, she introduced me to her friends as her lover, she kissed me on the rugby field. I had passed the doctoral exams with flying colors. Several professors praised my efforts. My parents had left for Italy again—my cauliflower head was finally growing out. In the margins of my notes to Wagner's *Tristan und Isolde*, I wrote, "11/11—the happiest day of my life." I was drunk with passion.

Chapter 6

—Until reality came crashing down. I called Robin every afternoon around five o'clock to find out when and where we would meet that night. This time, I could tell there was something wrong in her voice. She was no longer smiling on the other end of the phone.

"What is it?" I pleaded.

"I can't tell you over the phone. Come by my office. I need to tell you in person." How terrifyingly official she sounded.

"What is it?" The tenuous grip I had on reality was loosening. Obsession had a way of making an out-of-control life seem manageable. "I'll be there in half an hour. Meet you upstairs."

I slammed down the phone, put on my pants and a cute white turtleneck, sprayed on some of my Armani cologne, and went sprinting out the building. The stench of the subway entered my nostrils as I rushed down the stairs, practically knocking down an elderly lady lingering on the bottom step. I said I was sorry and pulled a token from my jeans and shoved it into the aged turnstile. In my haste, I did not put it in correctly. The bar smashed into my stomach as I tried to rush though. It knocked the wind right out of me, and I smiled at the homeless woman asking for money. She asked me if I was OK.

"Yes, thanks for asking." I gave her fifty cents.

The Indian guy selling newspapers on the platform was always on the phone. I wonder whom he was talking to, family members in Asia, his wife in Queens, a partner selling papers at the 59th Street station? He had a wide range of feminist publications on the left side of his stand. I usually spend a little time thumbing through the *Lesbian Lunch Break* for jokes and cartoons. I didn't like to read the heavy-duty feminist theory stuff because it depressed me. What women with consciousness need, I have always preached, is a better sense of humor. Otherwise, we are better off dead.

Nice small mice scurried under the third rail just before the Broadway One train plowed into the station. A descending major third sounded as the door opened, and the crowd of anxious students, who had survived another day of lectures, labs, and assignments, jumped in. I sat next to this extremely attractive Hispanic woman with olive skin. She was listening to Queen Latifah on her Walkman and tapping her left foot to the beat, which I heard because the volume was so high. I liked her because she had a definite air of independence about her. No boyfriend to lean on, no mother to go shopping with, nowhere she had to be in a rush. She was probably off to meet a friend in Brooklyn, Fort Greene perhaps, in one of those beautiful homes that sat on a tree-lined block. Reading a copy of Angela Davis' newest collection of essays, she looked up thoughtfully at each stop to scope out whether a crazy or dangerous person had entered the subway car. A woman that beautiful must always be on the look out. She never knows when someone like the guy who stabbed model Marla Hanson might walk into her life.

Robin's office building intimidated me. High-powered lawyers, investment bankers, and brokers were confined inside, running from phone to phone, meeting to meeting, like animals in a cage that's too small. As men and women in suits scurried by me with their *Wall Street Journals* under their arms, the security guys, surely sensing I was a lesbian, gave me the once over. I asked one of them for Robin Winter's office. It took them the usual ten minutes or so to look into a book for the correct location. They obviously didn't want to be bothered.

I got in the elevator with an older lawyer—I could tell she was a lawyer because she had no rings on her fingers and wore a red Evan Piccone power suit. I smiled at her in that special way I use to communicate the fact that I understand that she is a single woman trying to carve out a piece of the pie while giving up the rest of her life—vacations, family, friends—to achieve professional satisfaction. She did not look at me at all, perhaps for fear of acknowledging that she was a dyke too. The elevator dashboard lit up as we reached the 33rd floor. A long-haired secretary told me to take a seat. Robin would be right out.

I perused the Frank Lloyd Wright picture books on the coffee table. This must be their way of telling their clients that they know something about culture. Robin whistled and I looked up. She looked stunningly sexual as usual, and I wanted to take her shirt off right there.

"Come to my office."

I smiled at the receptionist in order to acknowledge her existence among these power-hungry careerists and followed Robin's Ralph Lauren scent back to her office. She shut the door immediately.

"Nice place you got here." I tried to cut her tension.

The office was decorated with pictures of men and women playing rugby. Photographs of Phil were tacked to the bulletin board.

"Listen, Jean." I moved closer to the inevitable.

"Phil sold his condo. He wants to move to New York to live with me."

I was in shock.

"Didn't he tell you he was selling it?"

"No, I mean, yes, but I never thought he would do it so quickly. I told him not to come. I told him I needed more time to think about it."

"Didn't he want a better explanation?"

"I told him it was a big decision and that we would see in a month or two. In the meantime, he'll stay in a tiny apartment. I feel so bad for him," she whined. "He is completely crushed."

"Did you tell him about us?"

"No, I couldn't. He will be doubly crushed."

"At least he would know the real reason, right?"

"I couldn't bear to tell him. You see, Jean, he can't live without me."

"What do you feel for him?"

"I love him."

"Do you love me?"

"Yes."

This did not seem possible in my mind. One person could not equally be devoted to two people. She clearly did not love me.

"How can you say that?"

"It's true, I'm crazy about you. All I do is think of you. I keep your sweatshirt right next to my desk so that when I miss you, I can smell it and think of you."

It must be love, I thought.

"I have never been happier in my life than in this last month, Jean. You have to believe that."

"Then why don't you tell him about us?"

"I can't lose him. If he finds out, he'll go out and find somebody else and get married."

"That would be the right thing."

"But we've been together for six years. He's been through a lot with me. He loves me so much."

I was starting to get very upset. The mixed signals she was sending me were feeding my insecurities to such a degree that I'd never have to eat another meal as long as I lived. Instead of telling her to take a hike, I convinced myself that I wasn't good enough for her. I had to show her how wonderful I was. I held her in my arms and told her that everything would be all right, that we would find a way to make this work. As long as we had love, I believed there would be a way out.

"You are wonderful, Jean. How could I live without you?"

I shrugged, not believing this to be true. Too many years of being criticized by Mamma and Dad. Too many years of being called a dog at school, too many years of fearing that I was a lesbian had resulted in no self-esteem.

I would show Robin just how little I had.

We kissed, and I told her I'd see her later tonight. She seemed happier as she introduced me to the woman architect who occupied the office next door. Nancy Traubman was definitely a lesbian. Just take my word for it.

Robin was different after that day. We stopped seeing each other every night because she was too busy at work. She went home to Pittsburgh on the weekends and didn't get back until Monday morning. She told me she had to get off the phone because she had laundry to do. She told me that she could see me only once a week or so until things got easier on the job. Like a calendar, I measured the passing of my life on how much time we spent together. Each time was heavenly. I never experienced the kind of sexual satisfaction that I did with Robin. The six hours a week we spent together felt as if I were on heroin; the rest of the week, I was detoxing. Sick to my stomach.

One day I got up the nerve to tell her that unless she told Phil the whole story and then broke it off with him, I would leave her. It seemed the only way to relieve the nauseous feeling I had been suffering for the past month.

"I will, Jean," she reassured me. "I will."

"When?" I didn't want to push her too much. I was too

frightened to lose her.

"Soon. When he is strong enough to take it. The poor guy has to find another place to live. I just can't leave him on his own like that."

"You are going to break up with him. Otherwise I can't go on much further. You promise?"

"Yes." She sounded sincere.

"Good." I felt relief the way a pitcher must feel after an inning-ending double play. I love you, Robin." But the nauseous feeling refused to go away. "I'll speak to you later tonight. You have to work?"

"Yeah. The partner wants to see the proposal this weekend. I'll be really busy."

I was forever accommodating. "OK, I understand. Call me later."

"Thanks." She hung up.

I hadn't read a thing since I reread the crap I had written in those blue books for the doctoral exams. I couldn't bear to. All I had been able to do in the last month and half was teach effectively; beyond that my days were spent daydreaming about Robin in front of the soap operas, thinking about how much Jack Montgomery was not the right guy for Erica Kane, biking around the city, talking to friends, and wishing things were better. Oh, I played a lot of sports: rugby twice a week and basketball with a group of women who played every Tuesday night in the Village. I just tried to fill up my time until the next time I could touch Robin. The stress was leveling me.

In the music library, I passed the time staring blankly into space thinking passively about what the hell I was going to write a dissertation about. I knew that I wanted to write on fourteenth-century Tuscany because it was an Italian subject (I would have to go to Italy "on business"), because it wasn't the fifteenth or sixteenth centuries, my Dad's specialties, and because I wouldn't have to study any German. But to be honest, the reason I liked the fourteenth century was because "fourteen" seemed to reflect the color red. I know this sounds bizarre, but I strongly felt red, my favorite color, emanating from the fourteenth century. While other disgruntled students worried about whether their thesis was conceivable, doable, or unique, I knew that my subject area had the right color. Now I just had to find the right angle.

I began to write Robin a letter.

"My dearest Robin,

I love you so much. I've never felt like this before in my whole life. But I can't take too much more of your indecision. You have to choose between Phil and me. I will respect whatever decision you make. If you want to stop seeing me, I understand. The gay thing might be too much for you right now. But just know how much you mean to me." Quite a pathetic and lame letter—which I never sent.

"Congratulations, Jean." I recognized Monica's voice from behind the wall of books in the library.

"Yeah, can you believe it? I could not have done it without you." I patted her gingerly on the back.

"No, come on. I knew you'd have no problem."

"I guess, no matter how hard I try, I think there is always a very strong element of luck in my successes."

"No luck here, Jean. You did it."

"Yeah," I looked down at her shoes modestly, the way fourteenth-century girls were supposed to stand in front of their fathers.

"Jean, are you doing all right?" She hesitated. "You look like you've lost weight."

"I've lost thirty pounds in the last month."

"You were never heavy anyway."

"It's the stress of the exam and being in love. A lethal combination."

"With whom?"

I had briefly forgotten that Monica was a homophobic lesbian wannabe.

"This guy, this architect."

"Where did you meet?"

"He used to come watch me play rugby."

I started feeling like a complete phony at this point and abruptly ended the conversation.

"Listen, Monica, I've got to go. A friend of mine is waiting outside for me."

"See, you. And eat something, will you?"

"Don't worry."

To tell you the truth, I had felt a bit weak in the last couple of days. I had chalked it up to fatigue and being lovelorn. But maybe it was something else. Walking across Broadway to go home and watch more television, I first became aware of an itching sensation in my vaginal area. What could it be? A yeast infection? Typical for most women, but I rarely got them. I walked home and immediately shut myself in the bathroom. My underwear was covered in a liquid, clear substance. I ran to the end of the apartment to ask Virginia, my brother's girlfriend, who was in town for a couple of weeks, what I should do. She was straight, after all, and would know about douches and those kinds of feminine cleansing things. In Italian, she told me that I probably had a yeast infection, like she gets all the time—I don't know how straight women do it. I'm translating for you now. She told me to get some over-the-counter medicine for it, which would take care of it in a couple of days. OK. Off to the local drugstore, we went in search of some magical potion that would stop what was becoming a terribly itchy situation.

Virginia was tall, dark, and beautiful in that kind over-processed "Euro" way. She wore only the best Italian clothes and, like Ivana Trump, would never be caught dead in a pair of shorts and a T-shirt. This was her first visit to the United States, and she was anxious to learn about New York City. This was hard to do, since my brother preferred to sit around after work and watch basketball games on TV. Virginia's eagerness was like that of any foreign summer-school student, but perhaps more so because she was leaving so soon.

The local Love Store always pisses me off. In fact, I don't understand the meaning of its name: Love. All I feel is anger when I walk out. I think that everything is too expensive, the women at the counter are not friendly, and you always have to pass too close to some big gross guy manning the front of the store. Virginia was enthralled by the bright lights and serious selection of products. I'll translate a bit of our conversation for you.

"You need a douche, Jean."

"I've never used one before."

"I do all the time."

"That's because you're straight."

"It has nothing to do with it. I like to feel clean."

"You sound like those ridiculous women who sell this stuff on TV."

"This will clear it up in a couple of days," she said handing me some Vagicil.

"OK, let's get out of here."

On the way home, I began to feel very uncomfortable. Once home, I ran into my mother's bathroom and grabbed the vanity mirror she uses to pick the zits on her face every evening. I placed the mirror between my legs and looked down. I sat on the john horrified. My vaginal opening was beet red and swollen. I shrieked, pulled up my pants, and called Rachel.

"Call Doctor Lubner. I hear she is very good."

"Do you know her?"

"No, but a friend of mine likes her a lot. Her rates are reasonable too." She gave me the phone number. "Call her right now."

"OK, but it's probably nothing serious."

"I don't know, it sounds pretty bad."

"All right, speak to you later."

"West Side Women's Femcare; can I help you?" a Hispanic voice asked.

"I need to see Dr. Lubner. It's an emergency.

"Are you a patient of hers?"

"No, a friend recommended her to me."

"Just a moment." Suddenly I was on hold.

"Dr. Lubner's office. May I help you?" This voice was friendlier.

"Yes, can I see the doctor this afternoon? It's an emergency. My vaginal area is swollen, and I'm very uncomfortable."

"Yes, she happens to have a cancellation at six thirty. How is that?"

"Fine." I gave her my name and number and hung up the phone feeling relieved. The doctor would tell me that everything was OK. I went back to the bathroom and inspected myself again. I noticed a small pimple beneath the thick pubic hair and rubbed my finger over it.

"What is this?" I said aloud. Probably a zit. In my family, bodily pain and imperfection were attributed to gas or zits. I remember when I popped that enormous pimple on Martha's back. Boy, that was a good one.

I tried to squeeze it a little but nothing happened. No white stuff. That's odd.

Virginia knocked on my door to make sure that things were just dandy. I told her that I was going to see the doctor and that if Robin called, to tell her I wasn't going over to see her later because I had to speak to a professor. She sat down on my bed and rubbed my shoulder.

"Jean, I've had a lot of yeast infections before."

"Lesbians don't get this kind of stuff. Maybe an occasional knee to the vaginal bone or soreness, but not infections. I'm scared."

The next hour passed very slowly. Oprah was boring. Sally was a rerun. The five o'clock news featured some girl who shot somebody's wife and then went to have her nails done. I don't have enough self-esteem to do something like that. I'd rather shoot myself.

I took the train down to 66th Street and looked for 1546 Broadway. People shoved by me with bright yellow bags from Tower Records as I circled through the revolving door.

"Femcare?" I asked the guard in a fourteen-year-old voice I had used when I bought my first Kotex.

"Fifth floor," he seemed to snicker.

The elevator was pink and smelled like baby powder. I was itchy as hell.

"Dr. Lubner's office is down the hall to the left," a kind Indian woman told me as tears began to roll over my cheeks. I shouldn't be here. I am not pregnant, and I don't need birth control. I'm just a mixed-up lesbian whose girlfriend is sleeping with her boyfriend.

Reality was making me sick.

Dr. Lubner's assistant handed me a pad and told me to fill out some forms. I went down the list as fast as possible, checking no for each ailment: heart disease, asthma, and fatigue. I didn't have any of that stuff. Yet.

Dr. Lubner came scurrying into the office like the wicked witch in Bugs Bunny cartoons. Hairpins were flying out of her hair, her mink coat seemed to be losing its fur, and the high heels of her shoes were coming unglued. "I'm zorry." She said in a German accent. "I'll be right wid you." Somehow I would have felt better with a tougher looking doctor. She just didn't look right.

The assistant gave me a pink cotton gown and told me to leave the opening in the back. I took off my underwear, shoes, and socks, placing them in a smelly heap that the doctor would not get close to.

The door burst open, and she said hello.

"Vat is zee problem?"

"There is something wrong with my vagina," I pointed to it.

She gestured for me to lean back and put my feet in the stirrups.

"Yes, yes, you hev an infection. Do you use birth control?"

"No," I knew what was coming next and slowly rolled my eyes in my head.

"Are you zexually active?"

"Yes." I had stumped her.

"You know you should be careful in zis day und age."

"I'm a lesbian." I said firmly.

"Oh, I zee." She seemed confused.

"You have a pretty bad yeast and 'tric' infection. You vill have to take antibiotics.

"Is that all?" I was relieved.

"That's all I zee. Make sure you don't zit in sveaty clothes after exercising. Don't eat too many sveets. With this medicine you'll be better in a day or zo. If not, call me again." I did not have the courage to ask her further about the zit. She slipped into her office and I slipped back onto Broadway.

I felt relief. Sure, I suppose I had some kind of venereal disease, but, hey, at least it was something that I didn't know the name of and could be cured with pills. Itching like crazy, I limped into the pharmacy on 77th Street and Broadway, passed the rows of shampoos and conditioners to the prescriptions counter. After waiting approximately six excruciating minutes behind a large woman in need of heart medicine, I placed my order.

"Please sit over there, ma'am. It will be ten minutes." The women pointed to some orange plastic chairs lined up against the dingy yellow wall. I sat down with my legs spread wide to lessen the incredibly uncomfortable feeling.

This is what Debbie on my rugby team must have been experiencing all last year. She had to sit out a season because of some mysterious yeast infection that made her itch to death. Eventually she completely changed her diet, no sugar, no yeast, and especially no alcohol.

I decided to pass the time thinking about Robin. Her voice, her smile, and now more than ever, her boyfriend. They had been spending more time together lately. What was their sex like? Was he on top? Did she really suck his dick? Did he lick her? My temperature was starting to rise. Then I began to repeat the most painful part. She said she loves me—how could she do this? She dreams only about being with me? How could she do this? I love her more than all the Alfa Romeos in New Rochelle and all the other women I ever loved put together (as Willie Nelson might like to say). How could this be happening? I feel alive only when I'm with her or when I'm about to be with her. The stars appear when we are together, and otherwise I stare at the pavement—a lunar eclipse could be happening, and I would never know. Last night she told me that she was going to see him in Pittsburgh this weekend to divide up their stuff. She was going to tell him the truth about us, come back, and start dealing with the present. I wasn't convinced. I was anxious. Maybe she won't have the strength, maybe he will convince her otherwise, maybe her parents will tell her that she is making a huge mistake, maybe I was losing my mind.

"D'Entreves," a strong voice called.

"Yes." I jumped out of my nightmare daydream.

I limped over to the counter with my legs spread as wide as possible, paid the lady thirty-five bucks, and made my way out the door. These pills would take care of everything. By the time Robin got back, my infection would be cured and she would be mine.

Chapter 7

I popped the pill, got into bed, and flipped on the tube. The Knicks were playing the Cleveland Cavaliers in Cleveland and they were losing 86 to 76 in the fourth quarter. God, they stink. How are they ever going to win the championship with Allan Houston and Larry Johnson? With all the money and arrogance of New York, you would think that instead of paying millions for high-priced bench players, they would develop some of their new talent. Nope. This game would turn out the same as the last three. The Knicks would stop scoring after about the seventh minute of the quarter, miss lay-ups, foul shots, and lose 110–88. I turned it off in disgust.

Virginia poked her nose through the door and asked me how I was feeling. I will translate our conversation.

"What do you have?"

"Apparently a combination of different things. A yeast infection, a 'tric' infection. The doctor told me those pills will make me better in a day."

Then I noticed tears in her eyes. "Come in," I motioned, concerned. "What's the matter?"

"It's your brother. I think that I make him sick to his stomach."

"What!"

"He sits around all evening and watches some dumb game or another. I want to go out."

"He just doesn't know how to communicate. I'm like that too. It's easier to sit in front of a ball game than deal with reality." She did not seem to understand.

"But he doesn't want to touch me anymore."

Oh no, I thought, a clear case of that D'Entreves family affliction. Their relationship is doomed. I did it with my girlfriends too, as you well know.

She crawled under my sheets and began to sob. "What should I do?"

"God, I don't know. He'll probably never change. Find somebody who will treat you with more respect. I have to admit that I have acted the same way as Fred in the past."

"Jean, you are so passionate about Robin. All you do is talk about her. You are so in love. You are different."

I knew this wasn't true, but I didn't try to explain why because I didn't know.

"Listen, go in that room and demand that he go see a movie with you. It's Friday night. If he doesn't respond, go meet somebody else."

She was stunned. "I can't do that."

"I'm telling you, he isn't going to change. You will be continually miserable."

My family was never any good at providing comfort to those in distress, especially those afflicted with pain in the heart. When I told my mother that I was miserable because I had just broken up with my then-girlfriend she responded, "Just pretend like she's your dog and she died." I burst into tears and ran out of the house.

Despite my good intentions to be different, I kept up the same behavior. I wanted to be a kinder person. A couple of months ago, I went to the gay and lesbian hotline office to volunteer as a phone operator. A room full of young men and two lesbians, obviously together, waited for the guy to begin the three-hour training session. First he asked each of us to participate in a mock phone session with already-trained phone operators, who pretended to be distress callers in order to see if we were right for the job. I left the group with two self-righteous gay people, a young woman with a chip on her shoulder, and a young man with a holier-than-thou attitude. They took me to the end of a long corridor, and we sat down in three chairs.

"OK, Jean, each of us is going to conduct a trial phone conversation. Respond as candidly as you can."

"Do you want me to take any specific kind of approach?" "No, we aren't going to coach you, we just want to get to know you."

I got a bit tense. This was all too intimate for me. The woman began in a high school-age voice.

"Oh, my God, I'm so upset. You see, me and my friend Debby, we were at home alone and, well, like, we started drinking some liquor from my mother's liquor cabinet and, well, I kissed Debby and shit, and she kissed me back and, like, well, I think that it was really sick. What am I, some kind of fucking dyke?" She paused. "Now you can respond."

Immediately a sense of anger sprung into my chest. I was appalled by this homophobia and completely forgot that it was play-acting. What does she mean by 'fucking dyke'? Wow, watch what you're saying. Would you say 'fucking nigger'?

So I answered, "Why do you think being gay is so bad?" I was later to find out that was the wrong approach.

"Come on, they're all prison-hopping, softball-slinging perverts, and I'm not like that."

"Well, I think that you have a bad attitude," I told her very innocently. "You should learn to be more open-minded about possibilities and differences."

The woman abruptly stopped the conversation and coldly said, "Jean, you're not supposed to answer like that. You are supposed to listen and be supportive, not tell the person what to do."

I was puzzled. I was just trying to help, and if I made her see that being gay was as OK as the flowers or the sun and the moon, she would obviously feel better.

"I'm sorry," I replied, "I'm used to being a teacher and telling people what to do."

The young gay man did not look impressed, and I suddenly felt insecure.

"OK, now Ron will try one."

He began: "Shit man, fuck, this guy tried to kiss me in the boys' locker room after football practice. We were alone after everybody had gone home. Does he think I'm some kind of fucking *homo* or something? What should I do? I don't want to deal with him anymore. He scares me."

I took a deep breath and started. "Well, how do you feel about it?" I knew they wanted to hear more about feelings and compassion.

"I just told you."

"Oh, right."

"I'm sorry to hear that you had such a rough time. How is school going?"

"I don't give a fuck about school. I don't want this *homo* bothering me again."

Once again my blood pressure began to rise.

"Now wait a minute, quit calling him a *homo*. How would you like it if people called you names? Homosexuals are people just like everyone else."

I could see the female counselor hang her head a bit when I started in on the caller again. "There is no room for intolerance in this world. Love is the answer, not hate."

By this point I knew that I had failed the test. I continued with my speech about intolerance, as if I was lecturing a class.

When it ended, I thanked the two trainers, told them it just didn't seem right for me, got up out of the chair, and made my way to the elevator.

I began to sob uncontrollably on Broadway. I couldn't listen and be compassionate. I didn't know how.

Virginia was sobbing when I returned from my short daydream detour.

"I can't live without him."

"You love him that much?"

"Yes," she nestled further underneath the sheets.

"I really don't know what to say." Then I had to stop myself from saying something cruel like pretend he doesn't exist and settled for "maybe you should talk to him about how you feel."

"I've done that. He keeps being distant."

At this point I did not have any more brilliant advice and changed the subject to what was eating me.

"You know Robin is with her boyfriend this weekend. She promised me that she would tell him everything and leave him."

"It's about time. The two of you are so happy together."

"I don't know, Virginia, I wonder if she really will do it."

"Of course she will. She loves you."

"I don't know about that."

"Don't worry, I'm sure of it." She was much better at the compassion thing than I was. Maybe she should have gotten that job on the hotline.

"God, I am so damn itchy. Shouldn't the medicine have kicked in by now?"

"It will—just try and relax."

"I get these waves of unbearable itchiness. My body discharges this liquid and it touches on my labia. It's killing me. I'd rather have three migraines in a row than this."

"Didn't she give you anything for the pain?"

"She didn't seem to be that concerned. Can you look at it?"

She crawled out of bed and shut the door to my room. I pulled down my underwear, lifted the sheets, and spread my legs wide. Usually when you ask someone to look at a wound, check your temperature, or take your pulse, you tend automatically to feel better.

"Oh my God," she gasped in horror.

"What?"

"I've never seen anything like that. It's as red as a tomato. You are so swollen. Oh my God."

I started to panic at this moment. Things weren't getting any better: if anything, they were much worse than earlier in the doctor's office. "It's killing me." I slowly ran my finger on the swollen surface of my vagina. I stopped when I felt the familiar lump.

"See that, Virginia? See that lump?"

She looked more closely. "I think it's herpes. Didn't the doctor say anything?"

"No, I don't think she saw it."

Virginia let out a small shriek.

"Jean, you have more further down, closer to your butt."

"Shit." I jumped out of bed and sat on the toilet. Spreading my legs as wide as possible, I looked down between them, and sure enough, there were more of them, red, raw and painful to the touch.

Virginia knocked on the door.

"I'll be out in a minute." Why hadn't that damn gynecologist said anything? I have fucking herpes.

A wave of discharge flowed over the raw sores. I have shitcanned my body. I would never make love again; I would never even touch anyone again. A tear filled my eye.

I limped back out of the bathroom and into bed. My head was spinning. I must have a fever, I thought. I felt nauseated.

"Virginia, please do me a favor. Go into my mother's room and bring me that fat book that's sitting on the night table. She is such a hypochondriac—she keeps this medical book by her bedside. Maybe it says something about herpes."

Virginia jumped on the bed, and we looked in the index for herpes. There it was, listed proudly under venereal disease. We read the symptoms carefully: sores, fever, headache, body aches, swollen lymph nodes, excessive discharge. Checking my body, I had them all.

"Holy shit. I really have it. I really have it."

"Listen, Jean, calm down. You need to be diagnosed by the doctor before you can be sure. Maybe it's something else."

"I don't think so. I have all the symptoms."

I ran my hands through my hair in defeat. Robin must have given it to me. Why didn't she tell me about it? She must have known she had it. How can a person not know about this? It's painfully obvious. She must have gotten it from Phil. I was out of control now, crying.

Virginia held me as we read on. It said to keep my hands clean and not touch myself if possible. Take baths when it becomes excruciating and pee in the tub if necessary because of the pain of the urine touching the sores. Take aspirin and stay in bed. Cover sores with zinc oxide cream. Drink plenty of fluids. Herpes can never be cured, but it can be controlled by keeping one's stress level down and eating a balanced diet. I slammed the book shut. Virginia tried to comfort me, but I was in shock. How could Robin have done this to me?

Rachel came over to keep me company. She brought my favorite Pepperidge Farm Mint Milano cookies, which I couldn't eat because they contained sugar. No more sugar for this herpes patient.

"Jean, I've never seen anything like that." She raised her gaze from my labia. You poor thing."

By this time the pain was so bad that I was in and out of the bathtub every ten minutes.

"I wonder if the bath is such a good idea," she said. "Shouldn't you keep the area dry?"

"I can't stand it otherwise. It's the only thing that brings me relief."

The phone rang, and Robin was on the other end.

"Jean, I only have a few seconds. I called to tell you that I miss you incredibly and am thinking about you. I can't wait to see you."

"Robin, Robin, I need to tell you something." My voice trailed off. "I . . . I love you."

"Me too. See you Sunday." She hung up the phone.

"Why didn't you tell her?" Rachel asked. I was in shock. Rachel held my hand until I fell asleep in despair.

The swelling lasted for three days. On Monday I went to see the gynecologist again. She took a blood test, prescribed some herpes medicine (which was of no use because by this time the worst was over), and told me she would call me in a couple of weeks with the results. I didn't even have the nerve to get angry with her for misdiagnosing me. I just felt sick to my stomach.

When I got back home, defeated, I called Rachel, who came over right away.

"That's a real drag. I'm so sorry."

"Yeah, well it's not for sure yet. I'm still hoping that it may have been something else."

"Are   you   going   to   tell   Robin   today?"
"Yeah, she's coming over after work. I don't know whether to

be angry with her. I'm just so confused."

"I can't believe she didn't tell you she had this."

"Anyway, she's probably pretty stressed out about the weekend with Phil. I don't know if I can handle listening to it. I wonder what went on."

Rachel sat with me for another hour or so, trying to keep my mind off of the herpes, reminding me of stupid times on the basketball team. At one point she lifted my T-shirt as I lay in bed and began to scrawl words and pictures on my stomach with a pen.

"Ti voglio bene Robin," I dictated to her in Italian, a beautiful phrase for which there is no equivalent in English. It is translated as I love you, but literally it means I want good for you. She drew a basketball and a peace sign and a star of David until I asked her to stop because I thought that I might get ink poisoning to boot.

"I've got to get back to studying Freud or something. Take care of yourself and get the story from Robin. Tell her you have to know if she had herpes and where she got it."

Rachel kissed my cheek as she always did when she left and made for the door. I turned over on my stomach and pondered what I would say to Robin. The shrill doorbell woke me up. I longed to hold her in my arms. I had missed her so much.

I ran for the door in joyous anticipation and peeped out the hole to see her standing there in a tailored Evan Piccone suit. There was the love of my short and stupid life.

"Robin, it's so good to see you." I held her tightly and stroked her thick dark hair. She seemed rather reserved.

"I missed you too—I can't tell you how much."

"So tell me, how did the moving go?"

"Fine. I helped him organize his stuff. Took my old records and other shit that I had at his condo."

We walked into my room and shut the door. The space still smelled of a sick person, and Robin asked if I was feeling all right.

"Yes," I lied; this wasn't the time to talk about herpes.

"How are your parents doing, Robin?" I was too paralyzed to ask anything but a banal question. She looked as sexy as the day we first met. That was only two months ago. Those full lips.

"Fine, fine.... Listen, I told Phil the truth this weekend."

"Wow," I really wasn't ready for this. "What exactly did you tell him?"

"I told him I was seeing a woman."

"How did he react?" I asked, trying not to sound too eager. I think that lesbians take a certain amount of pleasure in hearing about a man finding out his girl is seeing another woman.

"He was really upset, of course. But then he said something kind of sweet. He said that he could understand how a woman would want to be with another woman because women were so much more beautiful, soft, and sensitive than men."

I sensed a certain amount of sexism in this response but did not know how to explain my reaction.

"That sounds pretty progressive," I said, trying to be supportive. I knew Phil meant a lot to Robin no matter what their future would be.

"So then what?" I asked. Suddenly, I felt a wave of uncertainty envelop my body. His reaction was too calm, too calculated. Something was very wrong.

"Did you sleep with him this weekend?" I had to know. "Well, did you?"

She hesitated, looked off in the direction of the Hudson River, and said in a faint and frustrated voice, "Yes."

I exploded with rage. "What? How could you?" A spear was

planted in my heart. All the pain of the weekend—the herpes, the fucking gynecologist—gushed out.

"How could you? You said you loved me." Tears stormed forth.

"I felt so sorry for him. I wanted to comfort him."

"By fucking him? By fucking him?" I repeated those awful words, which meant something more real when applied to sex with men than with women. Even though lesbians talk about fucking, we aren't really doing that. Are we?

"Shut up, Jean, you can't possibly understand what I was feeling."

"What you were feeling? What you were feeling? Damn you. Damn you." I got up off the bed and waved my fist at her. "You have ruined everything. I can never trust you again."

She began to cry. "Listen to me, Jean. All I thought about was you during the whole thing. I couldn't help thinking of how you felt, your skin, kissing you. I missed our love making."

"Damn it, Robin, you sleaze. Was it just for the sex? Did you need it from him? Why couldn't you just talk to him, I don't know, hold him? Why did you have to fuck him?" There was that word again.

"It felt right at the time."

I was getting more and more worked up. I began to take all of her T-shirts, socks, and assorted clothes she had left at my house and put them in a plastic grocery bag. "Get your shit out of my sight. I want it all out of here."

"Jean, please, please stop."

"No, I hate you. I hate you." I sobbed uncontrollably.

Robin sat motionless in the chair while my heart broke. She did not try to comfort me, or say she made a mistake. She just sat there. Then I asked the most deviating question of all. I had watched too many bad movies.

"Did you enjoy it Robin? Huh? Was it good for you?"

"Yes," she said defiantly, "it was very sweet."

I was hysterical. I grabbed her by the shoulders and started to shake her. For a split second I wanted to slap her, I wanted to punch her in the stomach. I wanted her to feel the same pain I was feeling.

"You whore. I'll never believe another word you say to me. Love, what the hell does that mean? I grabbed the back of her neck and pushed her head toward me until her lips were grazing mine.

"Is this the way it was, Robin, is this how he made you feel? Good, did he? Good?"

"Stop, please, Jean."

I covered her eyes with my free hand.

"Kiss me now. Damn it. Kiss me now. Can you tell the difference between him and me?" I ranted, the words almost lost as I pushed my mouth practically inside hers.

"You say you love me, now show it. Let me fuck you now." We collapsed on the bed and I pulled her pants down to her shins. She unbuttoned her shirt and arched her back on the bed. Her nipples stood erect. I kissed her stomach, reached into her underwear, and jammed my fingers into her wetness.

"Fuck me, please," she moaned.

Chapter 8

The next morning we woke up exhausted in each other's arms. I still had my jeans plastered to my body. Never took them off for fear of exposing her to the herpes. She had not questioned my prudence. It seemed to fit the moment, the anger, the power dynamic. She was naked and I still had my pants on, like some guy in a Marlboro ad. Robin was getting dressed. I checked my watch: 5:30 a.m.

"Where are you going?"

"I've got to get home and get some fresh clothes for work. I have a busy day."

I began to lose control again, like Lucia di Lammermoor, who should have just died at the end of the second act instead of repeating the dying/fainting routine in the third.

"What do you want from me, Robin?"

"I'm very confused now. I love him, Jean. I love him, but I need to be with you. Eventually we want to live together. We want to share our lives together." She had said that at dinner the first night we met, but I neglected to listen or believe it, or something. Gathering her stuff, she bolted for the door and was gone.

Unable to go back to bed, I headed out on Broadway for a bagel. Dawn in New York City does not bring with it a sense of renewal like it does in the rest of the world. On this warm December morning, it is gray and damp, and the streets smell of garbage that has been left out overnight. Homeless people have retired for the morning, and merchants sweep debris into the streets. An occasional jogger headed for Riverside Park struts by. Did you ever notice that joggers never make the effort to avoid pedestrians when they run? You would think that it would not be too big a deal to move one stride to the right or left since they are running six miles anyway. What's one more step? Instead, they brush shoulders with you and scowl things like "eat my shorts," a particularly disturbing phrase considering their sweaty condition.

"Give me a poppy-seed bagel with a smear," I directed the Dominican behind the greasy counter. I opened the glass cabinets and retrieved a container of Tropicana Pure Premium and waited for him to finish. I cut in front of a daydreaming customer, paid, and walked lazily back home.

Then this absolutely screwy idea hit me like a moon rock.

I'll fix everything.

I'll invite Robin to spend the Christmas holiday in Italy. Six days away from Phil and her family, and she will see the error of her ways. We can stay at my mother's house in the Alps. We can go skiing every morning. I'll introduce her to my Italian friends. She will become intoxicated by Italy, the food, the wine, the sun, and the moon. Fred and Virginia will be there, my cousins, Mamma, and Dad. If we spend a full week together alone without her parents, phone calls from Phil, or work, she will recognize her true love for me. She will come back to New York, leave her old life, and maybe even move in with me. I had found the solution. This will work. I skipped all the way back home. I hadn't skipped since I was about thirteen, the year I realized I was gay.

Who knows why she finally decided to come to Italy? Maybe she buckled under my pressure? Maybe she longed for more violent sex? Maybe she just wanted to ski in the Alps? Maybe she would finally be mine?

At first she hesitated, said something about having spent the last six New Year's Days with Phil. I refused to take no for an answer. She had to come. I don't think that I could have continued my life if she didn't. Let's see. I explained: We will fly to Milan together, stay with my folks in the Alps for a week. Robin will fly back the day after New Year's, and I will stay a week with my family in Tuscany. It will be perfect. Just the two of us in love—and the rest of my screwy family. Before leaving for Europe, Robin will go home to Pittsburgh for four days to celebrate Christmas with her family. That way she can also see her family over the break. Four days of freaking out about what was going to happen while she was in Pittsburgh. Phil, the parents. It will be excruciating. She will return loving me less. Maybe I should cancel everything? Was this all a big mistake? She would never get over Phil.

The ringing phone woke me from my torment.

"Jean D'Entreves?"

"Yes" I said with some hesitation.

"This is Doctor Lubner from Femcare. The results of your blood test have just come in. I regret to inform you that it came back positive. You have herpes simplex I."

"Oh God." It was confirmed.

"If you have any questions, feel free to call me at the office. Have a pleasant holiday."

"But . . . ."

"Good-bye." The phone went dead.

"I've got to tell her now," I said out loud. I ran to find the car keys. I'd drive her to airport like I had done a hundred times for my parents. Virginia met me in the hallway and asked if everything was OK. I told her that if Robin should call, I was on my way down there.

"Be careful." Virginia sounded concerned.

"I will."

The gray Volvo was parked on the south side of 116th Street. It sat at the curb like an impatient grandmother waiting to go home. I zoomed down Riverside Drive toward the West Side Highway entrance at 96th Street. Mothers looked at me in horror, pulling their babies back toward the curb as I whizzed by. One even gave me the finger. Nice, Mom.

I screeched to a halt behind a stopped M5 bus on the Drive. A guy in a wheelchair was being rolled onto a platform, which raised him into the bus. I sat amazed, as I always am by the sight. How difficult it is for the disabled to live in NYC! People in wheelchairs are an invisible population.

At 96th street I made a sharp right-hand turn onto the highway. It was rush hour by now and cars moved in packs down the narrow roadway. The lights from the golf course in Jersey glistened on the Hudson as colorful joggers scurried on the path adjacent to the roadway.

My mother always marveled at those enormous white ocean liners docked near 42nd Street. She had come over from Italy in 1956 on the Michelangelo, and Dad had made a trip on the Andrea Doria, the voyage prior to the one that sank. Her heart filled with passion when she saw one.

"Those were the good old days," she would say.

My parents won the Ping-Pong tournament on one of their voyages. That was one of the most joyous moments of my mother's life, besides carrying her children in her womb.

At 33rd Street, the skyline of New York opened up, and the shorter downtown buildings came into full view. An old railroad track raised thirty feet above the ground wound its way through warehouses and abandoned apartment buildings. Whores found shelter underneath its blackened beams when it rained. The pilasters also gave them a place to run out of sight. I think that at some point, Donald Trump was going to transform the elevated tracks into a chic elevated mall, with restaurants, shops, and street performers. Tourists straight from their ride on the Circle Line boat tour of Manhattan could take a shuttle bus to the sight and take in some late-day shopping while milling around the forgotten outskirts of Manhattan. Needless to say, they scrapped the idea pretty quickly.

Traffic came to a dead halt at 18th Street. This was always the case during rush hour. When I finally rolled up to the Village, I saw gay men strolling toward the pier and kids with radios sitting on the cement barriers. Solitary cars combed the parking lot looking for young men, and guys from upstate sold Christmas trees on the sidewalks.

Christmas, I couldn't think about it. This was no holiday. My family was back in Italy, Fred and Virginia had just left, and I was alone. Robin was going home. My friends left the city to go home to their families. I was one of the few people I knew whose family lived in New York. There was something pretty neurotic about that because it meant that not even twice a year could I leave the damn city to go to Ohio or Philadelphia or upstate New York—where normal people were from. No break from city frustration.

The light turned green and I began to inch my way toward Chambers Street and the financial district. I felt the car buck several times, as if it were gasping for air. I pressed on the gas to no avail. The engine died. Horns began to sound behind me, reminding me to move. I flipped on the emergency flashers, put the car in park, and tried to start it again. Nothing, no sound from the engine. I pulled the lever that opened the hood to have a look inside, knowing full well that I had absolutely no clue about engines. It seemed like the right thing to do. Cars were inching by me, with pissed-off drivers giving me dirty looks. I opened the hood wide and peeped inside. No smoke, no fire, no wrenches, let's see, no donuts, no green stuff—antifreeze leak—I don't know, no hanky-panky. In desperation I looked up into the thick clouds and asked for Miriam's help. In a drone I asked, "I know I shouldn't be asking you this. I should save wishes for more important things like I hope my parents are well, or I pass my defense exam, or the Yankees win the pennant, but please, please, Miriam, help make this car start so I can get the hell off the West Side Highway during rush hour. I felt a breeze shake my cauliflower head, and I knew she had heard me.

I got back into the gray Volvo, took a deep breath, and turned the key. Without any hesitation the car started. I put it in gear, waved to the traffic behind me, and inched down the highway. I took the first left onto a side street so that if I stopped again, I wouldn't tie up Manhattan and be made famous on some six-o'clock Shadow Traffic Report as a "stalled vehicle blocking the center lane."

With the thoughts of Robin and herpes still pulsing in my veins, I snaked my way through the short, narrow blocks of the Wall Street district, still keeping my flashers on—just in case. I drove up to Robin's building and parked the car next to all the black limousines waiting for overpaid, self-important bankers to go home, or travel or do whatever they were wasting time and money doing. I jumped out of the car and ran to the front desk. Some young guy who obviously had a problem with lovesick lesbians, or maybe any lesbians, looked at me with a certain amount of disgust.

"What do you want?"

"Can you call up to Robin Winter."

"What about?"

"Please tell her that Jean is downstairs. I need to talk to her."

"Just a minute." He started to help a messenger.

I waited for what seemed an eternity until I reminded him again about Robin, me, and so on. He finally made the call after watching me suffer for another three minutes. I jogged back to the car.

In the rear view mirror I saw Robin come toward me. She did not look happy. She got in the car.

"What the hell are you doing here? You know how incredibly busy I am."

"I came to take you to the airport. But now I can't because the car . . . . There is something wrong with the car." I was starting to get hysterical and a tear gathered in my left eye. I always began to cry first out of my left eye for some reason. And I'm not even left-handed.

"I just can't believe how selfish you're being. I can't see you now. I have too much to do."

"But there is something really important I have to talk to you about. And I miss you so. I won't see you for four days. Can't you understand?"

"No, I really can't. Listen, I'll call you when I get home. OK. Please, Jean. You are being ridiculous."

"But Robin, I can't wait until then. I'm desperate."

"I have too much to finish. I'm going on vacation for two weeks. You want me to take work with me?"

"No, of course not."

"Then I'll talk to you later." She kissed my cheek, and in her short, black DKNY skirt ran back across the street. It was love, and I thought I wanted to die. I needed to be taken out of my misery. She was angry, she thought I was a loser-dope. Now she'd go back to her boyfriend. There was no more hope for me. Tears came flowing out onto my cheeks and the heartache that I had been carrying around for the last two months was magnified ten times. As the Volvo made its way up Hudson

Street with me in it, I stopped myself repeatedly from driving into the Hudson. Obsession hurts.

I parked the Volvo in the garage and walked out into the gray night. Robin's architect-friend Margy, a woman I had met in her office one late night, was having a Christmas party, and I decided I would go to satisfy my need to talk and think about Robin. They were all straight, but at least there was booze, and it was in the Village. A chance to get out. Margy was an unhappy, over-worked, co-dependent architect, who made large sums of money and supported her family in the Bronx. She was nice, nicer, in a way, than Robin. Robin really wasn't that nice a person after all, she was just sexy and demanding and, well, *hot.*

I had continued to lose weight steadily after my exams, and all my nice architecture-party pants were hopelessly too big around the waist. At home, I tried on three pairs, the crotches of which were at about the level of my knees. I searched my brother's dresser for a pair of suspenders.

I always think that suspenders looked good on women because they accent breasts. One needs to make a critical decision about their placement: under the suspenders (highlighting the height of the breast), toward the outside (giving them a kind of flattened, wider look), or toward the inside (giving them a scrunched-in, perkier quality). I opted for the outside, flatter, and, I think, more macho feel.

Never once contemplating taking a shower, I put Margy's address into my pocket, grabbed a bottle of white wine from my mother's stash, and jumped on the subway, headed for Hudson Street in the West Village. Margy lived in a renovated loft, just north of Christopher Street. Tourists mobbed this part of town on the weekends because of the many retro-clothing shops, the Tower Records store, and art galleries that lined Broadway.

Street vendors sold their wares in vacant lots and huge, trendy restaurants catering to people with vapid taste buds sprouted on the main floors of the loft buildings. I remember going to some kind of Cajun place with straight people once. I spent thirty-five dollars for chips and salsa, blackened fish, two mediocre Bloody Marys, and some down-home, country atmosphere. I felt completely ripped off, but I swear the place is packed every night.

Margy was one of Robin's best friends. Like most VPs in their office, she worked eighty-hour weeks, had little contact with friends and family, except over the phone, and spent leisure time drinking and having sex with strangers. From the day I met her, I had the impression that she was gay, not because of any mannerisms or overt love for Jody Foster or softball, or esteem for Eleanor Roosevelt, or other obvious tip-offs, but because of the way she looked at Robin. She definitely had a thing for her. I could tell a mile away.

I told the doorman that I was going to a party in 4B, and he let me go up. The lobby of the building made absolutely no sense. There was an oblong atrium on the left with leafy green plants and a long walkway that wound its way on the right to a yellow hallway and two dingy, narrow elevators. I'm sure she spends a shit-load of money living here for this hideous decor. I was clearly thinking and feeling my mother's thoughts at the moment. With her innate Italian sense of design and architecture, she certainly would have been appalled by the decor of this space.

I got out of the elevator on the fourth floor and made my way toward the party din on the right. With a demure knock—I am still not confident enough at the age of thirty-two to give any door a firm, stiff rap, for fear of somehow not being worthy—I announced to the party that I had arrived. Not that I knew anyone, I recognized only Margy as I made my way passed her tiny kitchen and the stack of presents on the dining-room table.

"Hey, Jean," I heard Margy's alcohol-altered voice scream from just to the left of the Christmas tree. "I'm so glad you could make it."

"I'm feeling pretty depressed, but I thought it would help to get out a little." This was not the time or place to expect comfort from Margy—or anyone.

"Can I get you a drink?"

"What do you have?"

"I have whatever you want." Doubt it.

"How about a glass of white wine?" I hoped that it was Italian.

"OK." She walked me to the kitchen and poured me a big glass of California something.

"So how is school? When are you going to finish?"

"All I have to do is write my dissertation," I said sarcastically.

"No problem." She slapped me on the back. "So Robin's home for the weekend. Huh. I'm so jealous of the two of you going skiing in the Italian Alps. It's going to be great."

Didn't she know anything about the pain and suffering I had been experiencing because of Robin's indecision?

"It hasn't been that easy lately." I was desperate to tell someone, anyone, the truth of the last few weeks.

"I know. She told Phil the truth about you two. Apparently he was really hurt."

Now I was supposed to have sympathy for Phil? Something was really screwy here.

"Let me introduce you to some of my friends. Some people I met at law school, some I work with, some are from Brooklyn.

Hey, Tommy, come here. This is Jean. She's a friend of mine. She's into music."

I smiled my smile reserved for heterosexual men. It was broad, yet with eyes bent to the floor. The package was saying, I want to look attractive to you, yet I don't want to give you any wrong ideas. Tommy was also visibly intoxicated.

"What was your name again?" he asked.

"Jean."

"That's an unusual name."

"Not really."

"It's a man's name, isn't it?"

"It's a French name."

"I see." Margy politely excused herself and left us to verbally duke it out.

"So, you're an architect, Tommy?"

"How could you tell?"

"Nothing really. I may not have my Ph.D. yet, but I am at an architect party. It's not that difficult to piece together."

"Oh," he said uncertainly. He didn't understand my wit; then again, neither did I.

"I work with Margy and Robin. It's a great place."

"That's not what they say."

"They work too hard. They don't know when to go home." He was starting to make sense now.

"Do you like your job?"

"I love it."

"That's nice." The conversation was definitely beginning to wane. I walked over to get a piece of carefully displayed salami and cheese and sat down next to the African-American woman on the living-room couch.

"My name is Jean, I'm a friend of Margy's"

"I'm Emma, and this is Susan." She pointed to her friend

seated next to her. I felt alienated at this point. I needed to talk about Robin.

"What do you do?" Emma asked.

"I'm a graduate student at Columbia. I study music, just completed my doctoral exams." Everyone was always so impressed that I studied music. They thought I did sociology, economics, or political science. Music was so impractical.

"That's great. Do you play an instrument?"

"Violin." The small talk was starting to kill me, like the detection of a small tickle in the back of the throat that would eventually turn into a major cold.

"How about you guys, architects?"

"Yes."

"Do you like it?"

"We love it."

"Oh." I was disappointed. Isn't there someone here who hates it? Are they all just a bunch of liars?

"Do you listen to music?" My old standby.

"I like listening to 101.5, you know that cool jazz station, Kenny G, Sade." Funny, that's what Robin always listened to.

"Oh." My favorite word of the evening. For me, the "Oh" response clearly indicated that I wasn't really listening. I noticed that my drink was empty and asked Emma and Susan if I could get them another one because I was going to the kitchen. They said no, and I made my getaway.

I poured myself another glass of California wine, which really wasn't so bad in the end. Mamma would not approve. She would say it's not as good as Pinot Grigio or Verdicchio or Gavi. But I liked this anyway, whatever it was. My next move was to check out Margy's CD collection. The very straight-looking girls in sequined dresses and low-cut blouses were standing by the window. The guys had on suit jackets and ties.

Though I felt myself being clearly heterosexist throughout the evening, I think these people looked really nice and wondered why lesbians didn't dress up more.

Margy's CD collection consisted of what I called the middle-of-the-road conservative collection. You know, plenty of Dire Straights, Bonnie Raitt, U2, Phil Collins, even the Indigo Girls because they are such goody two shoes. Nothing out of the ordinary: no Hole, or Belly, or Phranc. On the outskirts of her collection, she had some classical music: Mozart symphonies and Bizet favorites and Pachelbel's Canon. She probably owned these to impress her guests. That's what knowing some classical music does. It's like owning some nice china or an old Mercedes.

I waited for someone to come by and ask me about the CD's and my taste in music, but nobody did. So I waited ten minutes, looked through the stack twice, and made my way back to the bar. In the meantime, I heard loud laughter and looked up sheepishly to see the woman who had originally been wearing the powder-blue sequined dress dancing in her underwear and heels on the terrace with Tommy the dopey lawyer. They were piss drunk and whooping it up. I could hear people from the street egging them on, and I looked out the adjacent window to see that about thirty people had gathered beneath them.

Architects are so repressed—no wonder they lose it around Christmas. I sat down on the couch and watched the woman with nice breasts gyrate and felt very content. Maybe she's gay. Doubt it.

After about twenty minutes of entertaining the neighborhood and feeling the cold of a December night, the two walked back in and made themselves another drink. I told Margy that I had a splendid time at her party, grabbed my coat, and made my way to the door. That's where Tommy stopped me.

"Going so soon? The party has just started getting fun."

"I've got a busy day tomorrow."

"But it's Saturday!" He was slurring his words.

"I've got to feed my dog." That's when he did it. He grabbed me by the suspenders and pulled me close to him.

Nobody violates me like that. I smashed my foot onto his well-heeled toe then took a step back and kicked his shin.

"What the fuck is the matter with you?" He was shocked.

"Keep your goddamn hands off of me, you understand?" Margy came rushing over to see what the problem was.

"The crazy bitch hit me!" he told her.

Before she could respond, I gathered my wits and prepared for departure.

"Thanks, Margy, thanks for everything. I'll talk to you when Robin and I get back from Italy."

Fucking assholes, I said under my breath as I walked out into my late December Robinless dream.

Chapter 9

I woke up the next morning in a complete sweat. I had had the most horrible nightmare of my life: My mother invited me to join her for dinner, and when she saw me at the restaurant, the first thing she did was complain about what I was wearing and my hair. Pretty normal so far. We sat down and ate a lot until she said that she had to go to the bathroom. While she was gone, I went to find Robin, who was seated in the next room, told her how much I loved her and how much I needed her, and tried to kiss her. She pulled her lips away in disgust, but held my hand as if she wanted to hear more. I told her I had to get back to my mother.

My mother was not at the table, and as I waited for her to return from her lengthy stay in the women's room, the maitre d' brought the phone over to me. Dad was on the phone, very worried because we hadn't gotten home yet; it was already close to twelve o'clock. I explained to him that I didn't know where Mamma was and hung up.

I waited a bit longer and then went back to Robin to tell her how beautiful she was and how much I needed her. She rebuffed my advances again. At this point I decided to search for my mother. While walking down the hall of the restaurant, I heard a voice over a loudspeaker announce that there had been a terrible accident and that people were injured. I continued to walk down the long corridor, which turned into the wing of a hospital. Nurses and doctors looked at me in horror.

"What's the matter with my mother?" I asked. I answered, "She is faking whatever it is to get attention. She just wants me around her to take care of her as usual."

I walked on into a ward. The beds were arranged under tall alcoves, each covered with a dark-blue plastic sheet. I finally reached the space occupied by my mother, lifted up the sheet, and to my horror, saw a table with her head on it. Just her head, no body, no blood. I gasped. Her eyes were closed and her lids were yellowish in color. In a wheelchair in the corner was a woman who told me that my mother was asleep, that no one could wake her.

I walked over to Mamma's head and told it, "I love you more that any daughter could love a Mamma."

Her eyes opened slowly and she smiled. A tear formed in her left eye.

The woman in the wheelchair said, "I wish my daughter had said that to me."

And then my mother died.

Holy shit. I jumped out of bed and ran to the kitchen. My knees were shaking. I got some seltzer from the refrigerator and devoured a chocolate bar that was sitting on the counter. I've got to tell Robin the truth about the herpes. This has gone on long enough. The dream about my mother had made me realize the kind of abuse that I was allowing myself to endure. Mamma had used her health to manipulate me into somehow loving her more. If I did not love her enough, she would die, as she had reminded me so many times.

I went through my phone book and found her parents' number in Pittsburgh. My heart in my throat, I dialed. Her parents resented me because I had made Robin gay.

A pleasant male voice answered hello.

"May I please speak to Robin?"

"Who is calling?" He seemed to know anyway.

"This is Jean," I said.

"She isn't home. She has gone away with Phil for a couple of days." The father delivered the chilling information perfectly. I was floored.

"Please tell her that Jean called. I need to speak to her."

I spent the days before her return in bed, sleeping, nauseous, watching basketball games. She called me one of those delirium-filled days with some bullshit line that she was outside a department store waiting for her mother to come out of the store.

"I miss you, Jean," she said.

Oh, please. It was getting comical now.

I found a date Saturday night. I decided, to hell with Robin, she was fucking her boyfriend, I would go out too. There was this very attractive woman I played basketball with on the Tuesday nights. Her name was Anne. She worked for the city as a forester, checking the health of trees throughout the metropolitan area and responding to an irate homeowner in Queens, who desperately wanted to cut down the hundred-year-old elm because it robbed the front yard of sunlight. Anne seemed to enjoy the best of both worlds: a steady paycheck and a sweet job. By sweet, I mean one concerned with growing things rather than tearing things down, with green leaves rather than green backs. She was not in a steady relationship, and I think she liked me too.

I met her at Benny's Burritos in the West Village around 7:00, before the Margaritas-with-salt rush hour. I spotted her seated in the corner at a tiny table. She was sipping a Margarita on the rocks—no salt.

"It's good to see you," she said to me as she got up from the table.

"Yeah. This was a good idea." I felt pretty numb after the news of Robin.

"Do you want something to drink?"

"I'll take one of whatever you're having."

She signaled for the waitress who had shaved her head.

"She'd like a Margarita. I'd like another one."

"You look nice." I began the conversation.

"Thanks." I was intrigued with her frilly cotton shirt, which had delicately embroidered patterns on the chest.

"Where did you get that great shirt?"

"My Mom got it for me at a thrift shop on Cape Cod."

The evening was progressing smoothly. We each ordered the requisite burrito, vegetarian, of course. To tell you the truth, I don't understand the great love people have for burritos. They tend to taste pretty bland and generally need improvement in the form of large quantities of hot sauce. Yet burrito places are all over the city. I think customers are mostly interested in drinking the Margaritas.

I liked Anne's demeanor. She was so different from Robin. Calm, centered, understanding, she asked me specific questions about my work in graduate school and seemed rather kind and considerate.

She motioned to the waitress and ordered what I presumed was her fourth Margarita.

"You want another one, Jean?"

"No thanks, I'd just like a Coke."

There was a pause.

"Plant any trees today, Anne?"

"No, I spent the whole day walking through Riverside Park. In fact I was up in your neighborhood, making sure that the guys fixing the pipes at 104th Street weren't harming any of the new saplings we planted. They covered the poor trees with rusty pipes. My assistant and I had to move them to the street while the guys looked at us as if we were pieces of meat. I can't stand that shit."

For the first time this evening, I discerned a slight slurring of her words.

"Construction guys are the worst of all—though my brother told me once that delivery guys in trucks are the most disgusting when it comes to women. He worked one summer delivering air conditioners in Manhattan and said he heard the vilest comments hurled at women on the streets. The thought makes me ill." She paused. "How do you feel about dancing tonight? We could go to the Clit Club. Have you been there yet?"

"No.

"They have live erotic dancers."

"They sound good to me."

The check came and Anne plopped down forty dollars to my ten.

"I think I owe more than that," I insisted.

"Don't worry about it."

It didn't take too much for a graduate student to be talked out of paying for anything.

We walked arm in arm toward the extremities of Manhattan, toward the meatpacking district on 14th Street and Eleventh Avenue, where hookers and lesbians on a Saturday night made their respective stops for the evening. Anne stumbled on the uneven sidewalk.

"Are you OK?" I asked.

"Fine, fine," she assured me. I really liked Anne a lot, and she was helping me forget about what Robin was doing with her boyfriend in Pennsylvania.

A large woman with two interlocking women signs sculptured into the back of her hair guarded the entrance to the club.

"Just a minute." She stopped us short of getting in.

"This is always some kind of power trip. I don't think there is anybody in here yet. Too early." Anne seemed to know the ropes.

An attractive lesbian with blond hair, a white T-shirt, and blue jeans took five dollars from each of us, and Anne made her way straight to the bar. I was getting suspicious at this point.

"Want anything, Jean?" She was very considerate.

"Maybe a glass of water."

She got herself vodka with something in it, and we began to assess the atmosphere of the club. On the far wall were projected slides of naked lesbians in compromising positions. On a platform on the other side of room a tall, slender woman wearing a black leather miniskirt was gyrating to the music. Leather straps crisscrossed her chest. She sported a matching baseball cap that read "Baby Dyke." A flesh-colored dildo peered out from under the hem of her skirt.

"Can you believe that?" I asked Anne, who was starting to get that glazed-over look from too much booze.

"Yup." I noticed that she was sweating profusely, and her white cotton shirt that had looked so beautiful on her earlier had by now lost its shape and was pulled to one side so that her ugly beige bra showed through the embroidery. She made her way back to the bar.

We could no longer carry on a conversation. I started to feel as if I was being abused. Predictably, I did not say anything.

"Can I get you anything?" she slurred. I was repulsed.

"I'm going to the bathroom."

I made my way downstairs, passed the girls making out on the stairway. A pool table took up most of the basement floor, and I had to gingerly make my way around smoking women with big sticks. After all that effort, I was rewarded with a spot in a long line for the women's room.

The last time I waited in line to go the bathroom, I calculated the average time each patron spent in the stall. To my utter disbelief, the average time was one minute and thirty seconds. An eternity. What were women doing in there? OK, changing a tampon perhaps takes an extra thirty seconds, but it seemed to me that pulling your pants down, making pee-pee, wiping, and pulling them up should take a maximum of thirty seconds. Then I realized that time often is wasted in the stage prior to actually making pee-pee. It takes some time to get the pee-pee out, to feel relaxed enough to let it flow. As much as fifteen extra seconds.

I finally made way into a stall. As I was peeing, I could hear lesbians snorting cocaine and giggling in the next stall. So that's what takes so long. I took approximately thirty-nine seconds to finish my business and get out. The next woman waiting in line flashed me an appreciative smile. I washed my hands in the sink without worrying about germs.

When I got upstairs, there was no sign of Anne. I checked the bar, then asked the bartender if she had seen a women with short brown hair and a frilly white shirt. Just then I felt someone tap me on the back.

"Hey, Jean." It was Cindy from rugby.

"Hey." I gave her that big lesbian hug, you know, the one where you squeeze the person hard up around the shoulders to remind them of how strong and macho you really are.

"It's good to see you," she said. "This is my girlfriend Amy."

Amy looked like she was sixteen. I was horrified. Cindy was thirty-six.

"Nice to meet you. Listen, I've been on the date from hell tonight. I met this woman for dinner, and we had a nice time until she started drinking everything in sight. I can't find her. Maybe she left."

"Check the sofa over there." Cindy pointed to the dark corner near the DJ.

Sure enough, there she was. Out cold. Her beautiful shirt was wrapped around and pasted to her damp waist. Her jaw was open. I said good-bye to my friends and walked over to see her. Saliva oozed out of her mouth. I touched her lightly on the shoulder. She groaned.

"Anne, get up. I want to go home."

"Huh."

"Get up. I can't take this. This is really upsetting me."

She obviously couldn't move, let alone understand what I was saying. Her head sank into her chest and she was out again.

So I found her coat, put it over her, and left the bar without her. I didn't care if she ever got home. I didn't care if she was molested by maniac lesbians (a fear my mother had). I didn't care if she had to be kicked out onto the street and crawl to get a cab. I was pissed off as all hell, and I didn't care anymore. I left. In the cool December air, I hailed a cab and went home—alone.

Chapter 10

ITALY

Finally, the day arrived that my love and I were to go to Italy. Robin was back in New York, phoned me with a big smile, and said she missed me and couldn't wait to see me, and that we were going to Italy, and wasn't that great. I planned to take a cab to pick her up at 5:00 p.m. since our flight left at 9:00. I was sick to my stomach with joy. Because I was so demented, Robin's lies about where she was over the weekend no longer mattered. I would spend an uninterrupted week with my beloved in the Italian Alps. God, I felt sick to my stomach. Then I tried to calm myself because I was afraid I might get another bout of herpes. Ten methodical deep breaths. Ah, better.

The next part of the day was spent packing and preparing for the trip. I always pack a light bag because that is what my father demanded of me when I was growing up. He had spent the greater part of his adult life schlepping things back and forth from Italy and was very conscious of how much other people's bags weighed. In the summer it was easy to pack light, but in the winter it required a special skill.

My packing this time was elliptical. I ended up leaving out a lot of important things for the sake of space. But who cared, I was in love, and my love would shield me from the cold ice in the Alps. Oh yes, I was in love with a beautiful liar and cheat, who had probably given me herpes and could never leave her boyfriend. This was grand. She was great in bed.

Robin was waiting in the lobby of her building when the cab with me in it pulled up. My heart raged in wild amorous beats. I hopped out, grabbed her bags, stuck them in the back seat, kissed her, and pulled her into the cab. This took about ten seconds.

For some reason after I looked into those eyes, saw her again in some semblance of reality, I suddenly became very subdued. What the hell am I thinking, she had just spent the weekend with Phil.

"I missed you too," she said.

I held her hand through the tolls on the Triboro Bridge, the din of La Guardia Airport, a lonely Shea Stadium, and the intersection with the Van Wyck Expressway. Everything was so gray. Queens was the place new immigrants to New York generally spent their first years. It was truly the melting pot of New York, no matter what people in Brooklyn thought.

Robin and I did not speak much. I didn't know what to say to her. I was confused.

The cabdriver dropped us off at TWA. Hundreds of nervous holiday travelers stormed the counters. It was the day after Christmas.

I have neglected to mention anything about the fact that Christmas had passed the day before. It really didn't matter much; my parents were in Italy, my friends away, Anne was still passed out at the Clit Club, my girlfriend was fucking her boyfriend. I didn't feel drawn to Jesus. I was half Jewish after all, and since I truly felt in my heart that I had lived another life as a Jewish cellist and died in the concentration camps and probably acted a lot like Anne Frank, who, as you know, also was a writer, I didn't feel spiritually connected to Jesus or Catholicism.

After much practice traveling with my family to Europe, I was trained to use whatever method was available to avoid waiting in long lines to check my bags. The best strategy, next to faking an illness, is to spot a counter that has no one manning it and get into the line next to it. Chances are that sooner or later a check-in person will open that line: when it opens, you race over to be the first one there.

As usual, this worked like a charm. We had our bags checked in less than ten minutes. Robin was extremely impressed.

"Let's get a drink at the airport lounge," I insisted. She grabbed my hand and we proudly walked through the terminal. This was a pretty safe place to be affectionate since homophobes thought we were foreign; foreign women are culturally more touchy-feely. My mother and I always strolled through New York hand-in-hand—even after some idiot once yelled from a second story building: "You dykes!"

We sat down in the airport lounge, filled with smoking German tourists and a couple of guys from Holland. I could tell their nationalities from their accents. Again Robin was thoroughly impressed.

"We'd like three Bloody Marys," I told the waitress from Queens. She was about fifty and must have been doing the same job since the airport opened in the early sixties. I needed the extra booze in order to face Robin about her lying, and about my herpes. I finally had her trapped—the bags were checked, so she couldn't leave now even if she wanted to. She would have to listen to me and admit to her falsehoods. The trip was really about to take off.

The drinks came and in a matter of one minute I polished off the first Bloody Mary. Sufficiently drugged, I began the cross-examination.

"Where were you this weekend?"

"What do you mean? I was home with my family."

"Didn't your father give you the message that I had called Saturday morning?"

"Yeah."

"He told me that you were with Phil for a couple of days."

"Oh."

"He told me quite defiantly, as if he knew he was planting a fork in my heart."

"I can't believe he did that."

"So why lie about it?"

"I didn't want you to be hurt."

"I'm crushed."

"We just talked. We slept in separate beds."

"Bullshit."

"You don't have to believe me."

A tear began to form in her eye. She always knew how to make me stop. I paused for at least five minutes while slurping down my second drink. On to the next matter on the agenda.

"Three weeks ago, while you were home, I had an outbreak of genital herpes. Do you have any idea how I might have gotten it?"

She was stunned again. "What!! I've never had herpes. I haven't been with anybody but you and Phil in the last few months."

"You are lying to me."

"Fuck you."

Despite my misery and my conviction that she was lying, I loved it when she got angry. It was so sexy.

"When we get back to New York I want you to have a blood test to see if you have it. You must. Lesbians just don't get things like this," I said naively. There was a long pause.

"Why are we going on this trip? You should have told me all

this stuff before I checked my bags," she reasoned.

"I suppose. I was afraid that you would back out."

The waitress brought us the check. I handed her twenty dollars and told her to keep the change.

The loudspeaker announced that our flight was ready to board at Gate 203. I picked up Robin's knapsack and my own very practical bag and walked off first.

"I can take that." She ripped the knapsack out of my hand.

A hot dog stand selling four-dollar franks perfumed the hallway. We sat down in the corner. Robin crossed her legs, and I put my head in her lap and stretched out my legs. She kissed me on the forehead. This was why I put up with all her bullshit. I loved being cuddled in public. I craved it.

She slowly massaged my temple while talking about her last trip to Central America. I think she was talking about Mexico and a friend from college and backpacking and sleeping on the busses. She could have been talking about sewage in Queens and I would have been entranced. The sound of her voice was so soothing.

A steady stream of passengers, many with small children, filed by. You could tell the Italians by their Timberland shoes, their tailored denim jeans, and the cartons of cigarettes in white duty-free bags. What was it about this duty-free stuff? So there were no taxes. The merchandise was marked twice the regular rate. So where's the savings? The Italians also seemed more reserved than the Americans. Not in the mood for idle chit-chat and conversations that begin, "So where are you from?" My mother used to get incredibly nervous on these flights, so much so that she may have said ten words during the flight, two about going to the bathroom, two to complain about the food, two to say my father was a bastard, and two to complain about my hair. Robin was not saying much either. She was still processing our conversation.

After lightly poking several passengers in the back of the head in an effort to get around, we found our seats 26E and F. The check-in person had done us a great service by putting us in the right-hand aisle with no one next to us. Maybe she wanted to quarantine us.

"Great seats," I told a distraught Robin caught in her web of lies.

"Yeah."

We slid our belongings under the seat in front of us and snapped on the seat belts. Robin had to adjust hers a bit because it seemed like a heavyset person had last sat there. It was always amazing to me how the people preparing the airplane for the next hoard of passengers made it seem like no one had been there before us. By this I mean that there were no hairs on the seats, no gum on the tray table, no earrings in the little pouch on the seat in front. It always made me feel good, especially after I raided the freshly stocked bathrooms and stole the little soaps and perfumes. I brought Robin some.

"Hey, what's this?"

"I like to get a few before the other Italians take them all. These little soaps are amazing. They last longer than regular bars of soap." I finally made her laugh.

"Just sit down, will you," she insisted. I kissed her forehead and crawled over her to the window seat.

We spent most of the flight making out. I hoisted Robin onto the wet counter of the bathroom, pulled her pants to her knees, kissed her neck and between her thighs. She moaned with pleasure and I literally came standing up. A first in my life. During the movie, we huddled under covers and pillows and I sucked her breast while she massaged my back. I smelt her hair and she kissed my ear. I plunged my fingers inside of her while she held onto my neck. I told her I loved her and she nodded. I told her I needed her and she nodded. We fell asleep in each other's arms.

The European sun began to shine through the window as I raised my head slowly from her lap. I checked the faces on the family from Chicago, seated across the aisle, to see if they suspected any hanky-panky. The kids were asleep and Mamma was fighting with Dad. The tall, blond stewardess smiled at me when she passed by. I think we were safe. No one was suspicious of our lovemaking. Robin brushed the side of my neck with the palm of her hand. My precious *amore* was awake.

"These seats are uncomfortable," she complained.

"I feel great." I looked at her longingly.

"Are they going to serve breakfast now?"

"Probably a croissant or some ham and cheese. You want me to get you some coffee?"

"No it's all right. I'll wait for them to come around." I finally looked at her in the eyes. "I love you so much." I had never felt this way about anybody. Like a dog that had just entered the room, she patted me in acknowledgment, but never said anything. I forced myself to ask her if she felt the same. She said that she wasn't sure, but that I made her very happy. I guess that would be good enough for now. I had a week to work on her.

Breakfast trays removed, the stewardess announced that we were starting our final descent to Milan. We would be landing in approximately twenty-five minutes. The weather was clear, none of the usual fog. The temperature was 40 degrees Fahrenheit. We were on time. I hugged Robin and told her a couple of stories about summers in the Alps. She listened attentively and told me three or four kind of boring stories about some camp in the Poconos, where she fished in the lake and first made out with a boy. There was that boy thing again. I was not to forget about it. She wouldn't let me.

The pilot made a rather clumsy landing, causing several passengers to gasp slightly. I thought these things landed themselves. What was the problem? The pilot was probably on cocaine or something. The whole world is falling apart.

We taxied on the cement roads and were twice reminded not to leave our seats until the captain had turned off the seatbelt signs. I'm sure that the second reminder was for those Italian passengers who had a tendency to bolt to the front of plane as soon as it landed. I always had to quell my mother's natural tendency to push her way to the front. One day I pleaded for her not to do that at Loehmann's, the designer-brands-for-less store in White Plains. My friends and their mothers would stand there shaking their heads in disgust.

I carried Robin's bag for her as we deplaned. You can tell you're in Italy as soon as you get off the plane because of the overriding sense of confusion that hits you like a salami. First they put us on these Fiat buses that are designed to take you to the gate, with drivers who don't know when they should leave or where they are taking you. We spent ten minutes listening to our driver talk to somebody on the other end of the CB, curse, and say, I'm going anyway. Then, when he left us at the gate, the airline people weren't exactly sure which hallway we should walk through. So they sent some to the left and, after realizing their mistake, ran after those passengers and sent them back to the right. In the meantime, disgruntled American passengers watched in horror as their bags were dropped into a big pile in the middle of the runway because there was a baggage handler's strike. "Mio Dio."

"No biggie, Robin," I tried to comfort her. "We'll just go out there and get them after we clear customs."

Dark, short, beautiful Italian men in blue uniforms and machine guns lined the path to customs. That was a good thing about America, none of this heavy military presence at the airport. I caught myself doing the comparison thing between America and Italy. I quickly apologized to Robin.

We walked up to some guy who was smoking cigarettes behind a glass booth and handed him our passports.

"Where are you staying in Italy?" he asked us in a bored voice.

"Valle d'Aosta. With my parents."

"OK." He gestured for us to move on.

"That's easy." Robin seemed surprised.

"They don't care about you if you're a tourist. I think they harass the Italian citizens more. It pisses them off that they go spend thousands of millions of lire buying junk, like cameras, computers, and shoes in the U.S. It's also a kind of a racist thing. The carabinieri are usually from Southern Italy. I think they like to get back at their Northern Italian oppressors for keeping them poor. There is a natural mistrust between Northern and Southern Italians. Did you ever see the movie "Swept Away," directed by Lina Wertmuller? It's all about that antagonism." I was talking to myself now. Robin was staring at the makeshift arrows drawn on cardboard, which pointed to a door that led to the runway.

"Look, out there. They have lined up our bags in rows. Let's go get them." We moved passed the two hairy *carabinieri* guarding the exit onto the runway and made a mad dash to our bags. I pushed over a young kid, who was wearing a Chicago Bulls jacket, to get my bag first. He looked at his mother in disbelief. I had no remorse.

Robin grabbed her knapsack in the chilly, humid Milanese

air. I retrieved my black and red duffel bag purchased from Caldor, and we walked back to the terminal in search of the bus that would take us north and west of Milan into the heart of the Italian Alps. I told Robin to stand by the counter near the rentals. I would use my rusty, yet fluent, Italian to find out what time and where the bus left for Aosta. She agreed reluctantly because she liked to be the one in charge, the active one, the one in control. The smelly man at the ticket booth told me that the next bus to Aosta was leaving in an hour from Gate 2. I paid thirty thousand lire for two tickets, got my change, and smirked at him. Poor schmuck is staring at my breasts and he doesn't even realize I am a lesbian from New York City.

"Here, hold onto these. I don't want to lose them."

Robin placed the tickets in the front pocket of her new red ski jacket.

"Let's go have a cappuccino at the bar," she suggested.

"Sounds good, even though you know that I don't like coffee."

Italian coffee shops are like none in the world—not that I have been to the whole world. I think it's because of the way they are designed—so comfortable and cozy. There was a silver bar on the left, cluttered with brioches, croissants, little finger sandwiches, and red-and-white packages of potato chips. Steaming coffee machines spray milk into cappuccino cups. Coffees are placed two at a time beneath spouts, looking like a chicken's breastbone. Mirrors double everything to make it seem even more opulent. Guys from Morocco, or Turkey, or somewhere serve the customers. First you pay for the items you want. Then the cashier gives you the *scontrino,* or ticket, which you give the guy behind the bar, who prepares the order.

I brought Robin the cappuccino and croissant she ordered and went back for my Coca-Cola and croissant. Cola and croissant for breakfast sounds pretty barbaric, but I really didn't know the difference nutritionally between that and coffee and croissant. My uncle Davide always cringed when, at the dinner table, my brother Fred and I washed down our delicious spaghetti with pesto sauce with Coca-Cola. We should drink wine.

"Thanks." Robin grabbed the top of my wrist as I set the plates on the table. I kissed her forehead. We didn't talk much. I didn't think we needed to. We just communicated by touching, by looking into each other's eyes. The way honest-to-God lovers do. An hour of waiting for a bus with Robin was like having sex with her. I had no concept of how quickly time was moving. Waiting for a bus by myself, without a girlfriend, without being in a relationship, amounted to an eternity—like listening to the first movement of a Schubert piano sonata. I marked off in my mind that this was the first half-day of our seven-day vacation together. Somehow I knew I'd never be with her again.

The big blue-and-white Sadem bus pulled into the parking lot, and the driver opened the hatches to allow us to put our bags in. I smiled at him and made sure that Robin's belongings were secure. I was only thinking about her well-being at this point. That's what you do when you are obsessed with somebody. What am I talking about? These thoughts flew in and out of my mind like a trick candle on birthday cake. I couldn't put them out of my head.

A few stragglers boarded the bus with us: two male school kids from Turin, a grandma with bags full of food that she kept by her side, a mamma and a daughter with a pretty pink dress. Robin and I took two seats on the right-hand side of the bus, close to the driver. I liked to see where we were going and how fast. I wasn't one of those types who fell asleep as soon as the bus hits the highway. I wanted to experience every minute, every detail of the landscape that passed before me, every fast Italian car that whizzed by, every road sign that indicated where we were. I loved bus trips. Some of my most meaningful encounters occurred on buses. I probably realized I was gay on a bus. It was dusk on a bus from Genoa to Turin when I think it hit me. After spending ten days at the beach with my Italian friends and post-pubescent boys asking me if they could kiss me, all I wanted to do was kiss Victoria, the sexy daughter of the hotel owner. I panicked in that bus seat as the mountains separating the Italian coast from the plains grew over me like undesirable weeds.

I settled into the window seat, and Robin cuddled against me. She put her arm around the small of my back and her head on my shoulder.

"I'm exhausted, do you mind if I go to sleep?"

"Not at all." I turned toward her slightly so that she could rest her head on my bulging pectoral muscle rather than my bony shoulder. "Is that comfortable?"

The bus driver asked for tickets, and I noticed how different we were treated in Italy than in the States. It had nothing to do with the fact that Italy was better or worse. Because this guy could never entertain the possibility that we were lovers, he treated us with respect and kindness and no sense of disdain or fear. It was a subtle, but refreshing, concept. He thought we were friends. That's one of the problems with being gay: you think that everybody in the whole world thinks that you are gay when they meet you. It's so debilitating. I guess it must be the same if you are black in a white country or heavy in a skinny country. Even in the company of gay people, I feel different, alone, outcast. What is that all about?

The bus rolled out of the airport and squeezed by two pylons that guarded the back of the terminal. Italian bus drivers are the coolest because they drive a stick-shift bus, not common in America, and they have style. They exude enormous pride in taking a turn at just the right speed and angle, unraveling the steering wheel in a circular motion as if polishing their mother's finest silver tray.

My eyelids were getting very heavy as we rolled along the highway that joined Milan and Turin. Nothing much to see, yet. On this same highway was that hundred-car pileup, reported on CNN in New York. It was incredibly foggy that day, and some typical Italian was tailgating some guy, and he didn't adjust when the guy slowed down. All the other people tailgating behind him rammed up each other's expensive car behinds. Luckily, no fatalities. Just some fender-bended Alfa Romeos. Of course, this is much more of a tragedy than bent-up Oldsmobiles or Chevies on the Deegan. I am sorry for going overboard with my Italy versus United States comparisons. It's part of my family's neurosis. See, I can't help it.

Then, suddenly pushing aside my prejudicial daydreams, the snow-covered Alps rose out of the horizon. I am never quite prepared for this spectacle. It fills my heart with joy, like seeing Robin again after a couple of days, like the time Geraldine Ferraro was nominated for vice president, or like getting a first glimpse of my mother when she comes through customs at the airport. You forget about these feelings when you don't use them, but like knowing how to ride a bike, they never leave. I gently shook Robin. She just had to see this: Mont Blanc, the Matterhorn, and Monte Rosa showing off their majesty.

She picked her head up ever so gently and smiled. "It's incredible."

I waxed poetic. "We are going right into the belly of earthly energy."

"I can't wait." She looked up as if to say she was sorry. "You don't mind, I need to sleep some more." I stroked the back of her neck. She was asleep in a few seconds. I couldn't sleep when I was with her because, you see, I knew I wouldn't see her ever again after this week.

The bus pulled over at a rest stop. Italian rest stops are nothing like those patchwork mazes of Burger Kings, Roy Rogers, and Dairy Queens that you find on Route 87 in New York State. In Italy, it's like going to Zabars or Balducci's or some other fancy specialty shop. You can purchase the finest salamis, prosciutti, cheeses, chocolates, and Ricola candies, for those times you have a sore throat. It smelled divine, and though I could just kick myself sometimes for not drinking coffee (I have never even tasted a cup in my short and stupid life), the caffeine thrill seems to penetrate my veins with the smell of croissants and prosciutto. Robin had had enough cappuccinos for one day, so after looking and smelling all the merchandise, we made our way to the rest rooms, which, incidentally, arouses the same kind of anger I feel when entering most ladies' rooms in the U.S. Instead of reading "Ladies" or "Chicks" or "Gals" or some other sexist epithet, Italian johns distinguish men and women by using little symbols of a person wearing pants or wearing a short dress. Pisses me off. I indicated my dissatisfaction to Robin. I'm wearing pants, so I should go to the men's room. She did not seem to get quite as riled over this point as I did.

An elderly woman sat near the sink as we walked in. She had on a dirty light-blue apron and a brown mole on her nose with three hairs sprouting out from it. Americans just didn't have those kinds of moles. A basket filled with change was placed on the sink to her right. There was no way of getting around her without forking over a few lire. I guess it was only fair.

I handed the old women five hundred lire, which I thought was a lot, but by her snarl, I figured it must have been too little.

Oops. I consciously felt bad for thirty-five seconds and then fixated again on Robin. I needed something to be fixated on. We made our way hand in hand back to the bus. I loved this. I was never happier than on, let me record this day, December 26, at 12:15 Italian time. We made our way back to our seat. I kissed Robin dead smack on the lips, and the Italian passengers weren't fazed. Heaven.

My mother was at the truck stop when we awoke in the small Alpine town of Champoluc in the Aosta region of Italy. Surrounded by six other mothers, she waved frantically from below as we made our way to the front of the bus. I thanked the driver for the smooth ride and jumped down three steps into my mother's arms. I was happy as a baby. I was with my two favorite girls.

"It's nice of you to come get us." I hugged her. "Mamma, this is Robin." I could tell she was annoyed to have to focus her attention away from me and onto a stranger. She did her best to be polite.

Robin broke the ice. "It's a pleasure to meet you, Mrs. D'Entreves. Jean speaks so much about you."

"I'm a sure she a does."

"This place is spectacular." Robin pointed to the mountains to the north.

"Yes. Jean spent alla her summers here. But she doesn'ta like to come a here no more."

"Just because I missed last summer, for the stupid reason of having to study for my orals, does not mean that I don't like it here. Please." She was already irritating me.

"So how is Dad?" I asked another question before she could answer. "Fred and Virginia are here, aren't they?"

"Yes, they have a gone skiing. They will be backa tonight."

Then it happened. My mother had to say what had been

preying on her mind for the last five minutes. "Robin, you are a very pretty girla, but why do you have to wear yoo hair like thata?" She was speaking of Robin's new, super-sexy buzz cut from Astor place. Robin was in shock.

"You don't like it, Mrs. D'Entreves? I had it done special for the trip."

"No. It just doesn'ta suita you at alla. You needa something lessa severe."

"What do you mean?"

"Mamma, just stop with that now." I turned to Robin. "Last year when she saw me walking around campus in tattered jeans, I literally thought she was going to faint. She demanded that I immediately go home and change. I felt horrible. Just brush it off. You look sexy."

"So how was a yoo trip?" Mamma asked. This was a standard D'Entreves question. No need to talk about anything particularly meaningful, and plane rides were even more suitable for vapid conversation than the weather.

"It was fine. We were right on time. The only snag was the baggage handler's strike. Actually, I liked going on the runway to get my bags.

"What do you doa for a living, Robin?" my mother asked.

"I'm an architect. I work for a big bank on Wall Street."

"I betta you make a good salary."

"That's not why I do it. I really like my job a lot. It's a challenge."

"Where do youa live?" It was twenty-question time.

"On the East Side in a small apartment."

For some reason, I could tell that my mother didn't like her already.

"Robin's really good at what she does. Her boss puts her on all the biggest projects." My mother was not impressed. I don't know what she had focused in on. I surely couldn't see it.

"What doa yoo parents do?"

"They are architects too."

"Any brothers ora sisters?"

"Mamma what is this, an interrogation?"

"I justa want to finda out who is she."

"Well, can't you do it in a less antagonizing way?

Robin cut in. "Jean, I'm fine. Your mother and I are getting acquainted." For some reason, I didn't like this idea at all. Then Mamma would learn the truth about Phil, that our vacation and love for each other combined to make one big joke. She was practically engaged to another person. Mamma would make sense of the truth any minute now. I think she could feel the pain I was trying in vain to conceal.

"So, where dida you meet my Jean?"

"Playing rugby. We play for the same coach over the summer, the Irish legend."

"I hate rugby." She started. "It makes you girls alla have such muscular legs. Jean always come home witha bruises anda cuts. It's not a feminine ting to be doing."

"It relieves a lot of my stress from work. Instead of kicking my boss and my clients, I kick the opponents."

I knew that my mother was dying to ask her if she was gay. The only problem was that she would never in a million years say the word lesbian, or gay. So she tried another approach.

"Do you a like men?" she asked.

"Yes." Robin responded rather puzzled.

"I mean do you date a man?"

"Mamma," I jumped in, "that is rather personal."

"Let her answer."

"Yes, I like men."

This was all my mother needed. She knew the truth about our

so-called love.

"That's a nice."

We walked passed an old chalet, with its multi-tier wooden balconies dripping with icicles. Snow weighed on the rooftop, causing the inverted v-shaped roof to cave in on the sides, making it look like a mustache. The road we walked on was covered with a one-inch patina of white snow. And as we walked our shoes made a crunching sound—one of my most treasured sounds in the world, next to the crack of a bat on a ball at Yankee Stadium. Small Italian cars quietly kicked up snow from their snow tires. Our house came into view about a hundred feet away. "That's it. That's our place." I pointed with pride to the chalet on the side of the mountain.

"Incredible, Jean."

"It's been in my mother's family for two hundred years. She inherited it from my grandfather Guido." I was feeling extremely self-conscious at the moment. Showing Robin this house was like revealing to her some of my deepest and darkest secrets. Like the time I wanted to kill myself when I was nineteen, sitting behind the wheel of my parents' car, falling asleep and nearly driving off the Hutchinson River Parkway in Larchmont. I had some of my closest brushes with death behind a car or while drinking alcohol. Nobody knew that about me.

We walked up the steps to the lowest balcony and lowered our heads to fit through the front door. It was so warm inside. We immediately heard the crackle from the wood stove in the kitchen.

"I've prepared your room upstairs. You want to put on some long johns and warmer clothes? I don't know about taking a shower, though; we have very little hot water and we save it for washing our faces in the morning." Like any typical American, Robin looked shocked about the fact that we wouldn't take showers daily. But to tell you the truth, you just don't get that dirty in the mountain air. Walking around New York City for fifteen minutes in the summer will get you dirtier than one week in December in Champoluc. I swear.

We walked up the stairs and opened the door to the bedroom. Two narrow beds, with pretty flowery quilts purchased from Caldor and transported here by my disgruntled father, filled the tiny room. Two windows looked out on the snow-covered fields, and an animal head with six-inch antlers decorated the wall between the windows. The walls and floors were made of pine, and it always amazed me that these kinds of chalets rarely burned down. There was a greater chance that they would be demolished by an avalanche than burned down in a fire. An ancient dresser with four drawers stood on the left. A white porcelain sink cowered in the corner of the room. My mother probably had Dad bring over the white and beige rug that was placed at the entrance of the room. It definitely had that Caldor style. Somehow, though, through a natural sense of design, my mother made it seem to fit perfectly.

We plopped our bags on the bed. I grabbed Robin by the waist and pulled her near.

"This is were I grew up. Do you like it?"

"It's amazing."

"It means so much to me that I can share this with you. I love you."

"You are a lucky person to have all this."

"I know. I'm an incredibly lucky person." Then why do I feel like dying all the time? Robin went into some story about her summer at camp and tubing down the Delaware and barbecues and mosquitoes. I don't remember what she was trying to get at. No matter. We made out for ten minutes, just enough for my underwear to become completely saturated with goo. We put on some long underwear and our boots, fished out hats and gloves, kissed again, and made our way back down to the kitchen. The kitchen was the coziest room in the house. Mamma was making us some tea.

"Drinka this. It willa warm yoo up right away."

We sat down at the kitchen table, which was covered with a red-and-white checkered tablecloth that was probably brought over from Caldor. You get the idea. Most of the silverware, pots and pans, and glasses came from the same source. Our homes in New York and Champoluc were decorated from the same store. It gave our lives a certain continuity.

"Do you take milk, Robin?"

"No thanks, just some sugar."

"I like mine with a lot of lemon and a lot of sugar, just the way they have it in the refuges on the mountain." I showed off to Robin.

"If you come back here in the summer, we can climb on the glacier to the Margherita Refuge, the highest in the Alps, perched at 15,602 feet."

"You canna only go there with a guide," my mother quickly chimed in. Forever vigilant.

"You rent a guide for two days. The first day you climb to base camp and sleep the night there. The next day you get tied together, and he takes you to the top. It is the most glorious thing in the world," next to thinking that Robin was really in love with me.

We slurped down the tea and told my mamma that we were going to the local ski shop to rent equipment. It was about 4:00 p.m. Italian time, and we wanted to get everything ready for skiing the next day. I was a lousy skier, and I figured that Robin was too. Was I wrong.

We walked out of the door and down the narrow path carved

out of the snow. I put my arm around Robin. She slid her hand around my waist.

"Aren't you tired, Jean? Did you sleep on the bus?" Robin asked thoughtfully.

"I'm feeling great. Smell the air. No stink of oil from the New Jersey refineries. No piss from the beer-relieving folks. No grease from the souvlaki guys on the street."

Robin stared up at the peaks that surrounded the little town of Champoluc like a tourist on Fifth Avenue looking at the skyscrapers.

"Have you climbed all these peaks?"

"Most of them. They are really not that dangerous. The trails are very steep and incredibly windy. The views are spectacular from the top. On a clear day you can see all the way to Turin."

"I'd like to climb them sometime."

I knew this was never going to happen.

The ski shop was owned by my mother's best friend, Marilena. They grew up together, spending the summers playing jokes on the local imbecile and stealing tomatoes from an old lady. I saw photographs of them on a New Year's Eve morning, piss drunk, holding onto a telephone pole and smoking cigarettes. Marilena had two kids too, a girl and a boy. I think that families with only one girl and one boy tend to be fucked-up. That is because a weird power dynamic develops between Mamma and daughter and Papa and son. In the car going on long trips, I always sat behind my mother, Fred behind Dad. They talked about boy things, we talked about girl things. There is jealousy between the parents for the children's attention and vice versa. I think an extra child thrown into the mix would make things a lot healthier.

The ski shop was vintage Italy. Every article, whether a postcard, a pair of Rossignol skis, a Fila jacket, or a silly souvenir pocketknife, had style that you couldn't find in America. Everything was carefully displayed, and every inch of the store filled with merchandise. We walked into the store, and a loud cheer of "guardi chi si vede" (look who's here) erupted when they saw me. It was like this every year, and it made me feel good. I tended to forget about my friends in Italy when I was away. But they never disappeared. I hugged the four members of the family, who interrupted a customer to greet me. I introduced Robin as my friend. She was not particularly amiable to them. Probably felt a little nervous. After telling them about my schoolwork and hearing about how much my mother was waiting for me to arrive, they led us to the back room to be fitted for skis, boots, poles, and other accessories.

The last time I went skiing was with Martha in the Adirondacks, and that was a whole different thing. The ski-rental place was like a factory, and the customers like chassis assembled on conveyor belts. In long lines we were moved from station to station. At each stop we were fitted with some ski thing or another until we reached the end, where we had all the equipment necessary to go out onto the slopes. Here, it was a family affair. We chatted with the son as he asked us which kind of boot we preferred, which ski, what height. He smiled at us and asked some questions about New York, and whether we liked Italy better than New York. I always got that.

We thanked the son and gathered all the junk we had just rented. If you are not a skier, this is the most difficult and arduous task. Robin balanced the skis and poles over her shoulder and carried the boots in her right hand. My poles were sliding all over the place, clanking to the ground. The skis slid back and forth on my jacket. We had to stop three times to adjust things, until Robin said that she could carry my skis too. No way. I would never allow a girlfriend of mine to carry anything. I had more pride than that.

We finally made it back to the house, my shoulders aching and the back of my neck red from the several times I had hit it with the poles. Mamma had dutifully prepared us our dinner of spaghetti and a piece of meat. We placed the skis in the garage and sat down immediately to eat. Dad joined us for the first time. I hugged him hello and introduced him to Robin.

"Nice to meet you, Dr. D'Entreves," Robin said politely. I knew instinctively that they would get along. They were made of the same self-involved and insecure fiber. Dad immediately asked her what she did and seemed impressed. Robin went into some long harangue about a design she was working on. My mother and I exchanged glances.

"Where's Fred?" I asked her.

"He is having dinner at Virginia's parents' house."

"How are they doing? They fought a lot in New York. Virginia seemed frustrated."

"They fight all the time. I think that they are both a little crazy. She as much as he."

"I guess. I wonder whether Fred will ever find the right person."

Robin was still blabbing happily with Dad. They were like two pigs in shit.

"Mamma, this food is so delicious. The most innocent ingredients, butter, oil, are better than anything you can get in America."

"Youa better likea it." Mamma looked at me with a worried look. "Where dida you meet her, Jean?" she said sotto voce.

"I told you. Playing rugby."

"There isa something about her I a don really like."

"What do you mean? You just met her!"

"Are youa telling me the truth abouta her?" I was dying to

tell my mother about the boyfriend, the herpes, the pain, but I just couldn't because she would do the most logical thing and put Robin's sorry ass on the next flight to New York. "You just don't look right, Jean. Not happy." She shook her head. "You are too skinny."

Robin thanked my parents for inviting her to stay. Of course it never occurred to her to bring a gift. My mother would pick up on that right away. We told Mamma to relax and go into the living room and we would take care of the dishes. Robin washed and I dried.

"Your Dad seems like a really great guy, really charming." Robin smiled. "He is so smart."

"I guess that he is pretty accomplished, having written all those books. His students love him too." I paused. "He can be such a dick though." I had to remove the spotlight from him.

"It certainly doesn't seem like it." She defended him.

"Well, you're not his son or daughter. Take my word for it, he can be really mean. He is much nicer to strangers and his students than to his own family." I couldn't tell if I was jealous of Dad or not. Or angry at Robin. "Let's just get off the subject," I suggested.

By now it was close to six o'clock and I could barely keep my eyes open. We sat down with the folks for ten more dreadful minutes, excused ourselves, brushed our teeth, washed our faces in the bedroom sink, shivered, and jumped under the goose down comforter in one narrow Italian bed.

"I've never slept without any clothes on in Italy before. In fact," I began to kiss her neck, "I have never made love in Italy before."

"I thought you said you were exhausted."

"I'm starting to get my second wind."

"I see."

Our lovemaking that night was violent as usual. I placed Robin in whatever way I pleased. I held her down tight and rammed myself into her. I was so angry and frustrated. We came over and over again, each time flipping off the covers momentarily to dry off our sweat. And then, as easily as we gave in to one another's passion, we fell soundly asleep.

Chapter 11

The next day the sun peeked through the cracks between the wooden shutters and made its way to my left eye as I held Robin close to my breast. I rolled over. She awoke. That moment when your lover awakes after a long sleep is one of life's most incredible moments. Isn't it? Shouldn't it be? I kissed her gently on the forehead.

"Good morning, my darling," I whispered in her ear.

"Good morning, Jean." She wiped the drool from the corner of her lip. "What time is it?"

"Let's forget about time. Let's lie in bed all day. We have never done that before."

"Don't you want to go skiing?"

"That can wait." I started to feel panicky.

"Just tell me what time it is. My watch is on the night stand." She reached over me to get at it.

"No, you can't know." I lunged at it before she reached it.

"Stop being silly, Jean. I want to get up and do things." She was really getting irritated. I could tell because the horizontal crease on her forehead deepened.

"All right, all right." I glanced down to see that it was 1:35 p.m. Italian time. Oh no, she would be angry.

"It's one o'clock." I said, using my mother's method of calculating time. Time was measured according to what and when you needed your kids to do something for you. If they had to get up right away, then it was half an hour faster than actual time. If she wanted us to stay longer for dinner, it was a half an hour slower. What was time anyway but some thirteenth-century invention? It's really relative, you know.

"I slept for twelve hours. I was pooped," Robin explained. "Let's go skiing." Without as much as a kiss hello, or a final embrace and ensuing orgasm, she jumped out of bed, put on a long T-shirt, her nipples standing up in the cold air, and walked right out the door to the bathroom. I began to cry. What did I want from this person? She was not my girlfriend, she just wanted sex, or companionship, or something. She was not crazy about me the way I was about her. I could not eat, sleep, drink, or feel anything without thinking of her. She was my breath and my nourishment, my mother and father, my friends. She was my work, since I had completely given up working on my dissertation. What was my subject again, fourteenth-century Lucca? Who cares? Who the fuck cares? All I wanted was to fuck Robin. Fuck my Ph.D.

She walked back in the room smelling of toothpaste. Her dark hair was slightly wet near the scalp where she had washed off the soap. She began to put on her bra and her long johns and, well, prepared to go skiing. "It's a beautiful day, Jean. Get up. I didn't come all the way to the Italian Alps to lie in bed."

"Come here, first. Let me kiss you one more time."

"OK, but just once." That sounded like a line she would say to Phil. He must be just as neurotic as me in these last months, competing with an unknown quantity of woman in New York.

After the kiss, I put on a flannel shirt and ran to the bathroom to wash up. Italian bathrooms are so great. It's a treat to figure out just what is what. First thing to decode is which of the five different light switches near the door turns on which light because the bathroom switches also turn on the hall and the stair lights. The bottom switch actually turns on the main bathroom light, while the middle one turns on the light above the sink, and of course, the top one turns on the front door lights. Must have been an ambitious day for the electrician.

My mother had decorated the downstairs bathroom in red. The tile on the floor was red, the bath mat from Caldor was red, the fuzzy thing around the wooden flap of the toilet was red, and all the plastic accouterments, including the toothbrush holder and soap dish, were red. I sat down on the icy plastic bowl, which is, incidentally, narrower than an American equivalent. Now the tricky part for foreigners: how do you flush the toilet? Do you pull a cord, press a button, or depress a lever? It was always a great adventure. In my mother's bathroom, you pressed a button on the tank that loomed above the toilet. Like a bursting dam in the Alps, the water came down with such force that it actually spilled over the edge onto the floor. I was ready for it and stepped away just in time.

I walked over to the sink, turned on the Alpine glacier water, and rubbed my hands in it. Now you may think that this is so easy. Actually, in most Italian bathrooms you have to figure out just how to get the water into the sink. Italian designers have invented all sorts of different ways to get hot and cold water from out of the ground and somewhere into the sink. One, two, or sometimes three spouts. Gold-, silver-, or ceramic-colored triangular, square, or round knobs. No indication of hot and cold—that was generally part of the fun. We had two spouts with knobs that had to be gently pulled up to gauge how much water you wanted. Then the hot and cold water would mix into the porcelain sink. A wonderful design.

I brushed my teeth with Italian toothpaste, which tastes like licorice, not peppermint like American pastes. I love it. It's thicker than Crest and feels better on the teeth. Then I washed my face with some soap, which I'm pretty sure my mother brought from the Love Store in Manhattan. Alas, Italian soaps aren't that great. They don't make enough lather. I brushed my cauliflower head with an Italian hair brush, which I had brought with me from New York. It's the only thing that will penetrate my thick locks.

Relatively clean, I rushed up the stairs to find my lady love in a ski suit, adjusting her sunglasses.

"You're really ready to go? Don't you want to eat something first?

"No, there must be something to get on the slopes. I'm dying to get out there. It's spectacular."

I think I was really stalling for time. I hadn't been skiing in Champoluc for at least ten years, and to tell you the truth, I was scared. The trails are difficult. There were treacherous sections with orange plastic fences that prevent you from falling into a gorge. A stretch of the trail even runs along the main highway. What was I getting myself into just to spend a week with my beloved Robin? I put on a sixties pair of spandex black ski pants borrowed from my uncle Davide (he is six feet tall and weighs 200 pounds), an extra-large turtleneck, and an itchy, bright red sweater, which did not itch my skin because I had too many layers on. I looked like Robert Redford in that ski movie. What was it called? Capping off the outfit was a really stupid thick green and orange hat left over from junior high days. I never had the heart to trash that hat because it was in really good shape. It didn't look tattered or frayed around the edges. It must be the rayon or polyurethane or whatever it's made of.

Robin was downstairs chatting up a storm with my father when I got down to the kitchen. Dad never spoke to me for such a long and intensive period of time. I'm telling you, he was always better with his students than with his family.

"Did you have some coffee, Robin?"

"Yes, your father and I had some espresso. Great stuff."

"I've never touched it in my life, as you all know. The thought of coffee makes me nauseous." I tried to disrupt the flow of their conversation.

"Then your client wanted the marble floors from Carrara?" Dad resumed. "Isn't that expensive?"

"So, Dad, how's your new book coming?" I interrupted again, insanely jealous of the entire situation, Robin talking so frankly to Dad and Dad spending time talking to Robin. He thought she was sexy—I'm sure.

"OK," Dad acknowledged my presence. I had finally managed to halt their conversation, like shutting the faucet so tightly that the leak stopped. "I think it will be done in a month."

"What is it about?" Robin asked in the most interested tone I had ever heard her use. I am extremely tuned in to these kinds of things. After all, I was getting my Ph.D. in music.

"I'm writing a book on Italian writers and anorexia nervosa: the anorexic as the prototypical figure in Italian twentieth-century literature," Dad revealed. I knew she would be incredibly impressed.

"That's a great idea. What have you discovered?"

"Oh." He paused to gather in her compliment. He was so modest. "Writers subconsciously described beauty as skinny, frail, and dysfunctional."

"Fascinating," she gasped.

"Quite," I said sotto voce. Dad had a willing and able audience at his disposal. They talked while I made myself a cup of herbal tea, drank it, rinsed the cup, fixed my hair, sat in the living room looking at the old picture book of the Kennedy family that we had on the shelf (it always made my cry), walked back in and out of the kitchen, looking for an imaginary pen or pencil, and sat back down on the sofa. Finally Robin walked into the room.

"He is really interesting." She gleamed.

"I know, isn't he charming?" I said halfheartedly.

"Don't be sarcastic. You're lucky to have a father like that," she said.

"Not everybody would agree with you." I stood my ground against the two of them.

"Are you ready?" she asked.

"I have been for the last twenty minutes."

"Let's go." She checked her watch. "It's already a quarter to three."

"I know," I said, like some little seven-year-old who says I know to everything you try to explain to her.

We put on our sun glasses, hats and gloves, said good-bye to my father, still seated on his throne in the kitchen, opened the front door, and let the light flood into our eyes. It was not particularly cold in the snow, not like it is in Vermont or upstate New York, where the wind swoops across the snow straight into your heart. I could never understand how people in their right minds could go skiing in those cold conditions. I told Robin that. She thought I sounded bitchy. Now she was used to my father's eloquence. I was doomed. I couldn't hold a candle to him, of course.

We put on our ski boots in the garage and left our sneakers in a pile in the corner. Then she piled her poles and skis neatly on her shoulder as I tried to get mine up there, each time one pole sliding off, like the novice waitress who lets a dirty knife slide off the plate onto the lap of the patron. Robin patiently helped me scoop it back on my shoulder. And I thanked her wholeheartedly. I was completely out of whack and unnerved at the moment. Whatever little self-esteem I had left after the events of the fall had disappeared. I had lost my soul.

"God, I'm such a spaz. I can't seem to carry these things correctly. I'm really sorry," I admitted.

"Sorry for what? You're doing fine." Robin did comfort me.

We walked over to the chairlift, submerged in a crowd of people. We plopped our ski gear on the packed snow and began to prepare for the ascent. First I tightened the buckles on Robin's boots, and then she tightened mine. Then I watched her gingerly snap her boots into the bindings, then I did mine with a little help from her. Then we put both poles in our right hand and headed to the end of the line, which wasn't a line at all: it was more like a hoard. Italians don't make lines, especially at the bank, where it's particularly annoying to have people's elbows on the marble ledge while you are talking to the teller. Robin seemed shocked by this lack of organization.

"Forget the moralizing, Robin. Just concentrate on squeezing in front of this family while they're not looking." Creating one's own sense of space in this throng of people seemed a lot easier with a pair of skis on because the length of the skis themselves made space ahead and behind. I think this made for less tension than, let's say, getting into the stadium where an Italian soccer game is about to be held. I tried to make a couple of jokes about the fact that there were no lines, but Robin didn't laugh.

"This is so ridiculous," Robin said in exasperation.

"Just keep inching forward—we're getting there. And anyway, Robin, why don't you explain the technique to me about how to get on the lift. Do you stand still or get a sliding start as the chair comes at you? I'm nervous about getting on. I've had some particularly traumatic experiences, when I was about seven, of falling off the tee bar and sinking in the depths of the snow, only to be pulled out by some pissed-off instructor who was having a bad day."

"You don't move. Just point your skis straight ahead of you. Hold your poles firmly, and the guy will slip the chair under your butt. Keep your knees loose though. You don't want them to get stuck. You can sprain a knee pretty easily."

"Gee, I hope that doesn't happen. Would ruin things, huh? I have that sore knee from last summer. Remember?" I asked her.

"You don't talk about that much. How does it feel, anyway?

"OK, sort of. It's still a little tender." It was a little late to worry about the knee. I was determined to have a good time with the love of my life. Nothing would stop me.

We gave the tickets to the Italian ticket collector and slid into position. I slid off too much to the right and had to quickly hop back into position. We squatted a bit in preparation for the chair, and smack, the damn thing hit the back of my leg, and we slid on.

"Not bad, Jean," Robin seemed satisfied. I could feel the blood coagulate at the impact site, but did not say a word.

We let our skis dangle into the ice-filled air. Climbing at a steep angle, hugging the slope, we could reach out and touch the snow if we wanted. The sun was directly behind us, warming our necks and backs.

"When I was a kid, my dog Bobby used to try and follow my brother and me up this slope. After about ten feet of climbing through five feet of snow, he would think better of it and return to my mother. I loved that he tried to follow us."

Robin then told me one of her dog stories. I listened to it patiently, even though it wasn't nearly as cute as mine was. Do you ever notice that certain people don't listen to the stories you tell? I think that Robin was usually thinking of another story she could tell while I was telling mine. There is a story in the *Decameron* by Boccaccio, I think it is Day 4, story 1, where the moral is that the ability to tell a good story is like having sex, "coming" together, meaning that both parties enjoyed the climax. I wasn't experiencing nearly the same pleasure during this storytelling as Robin was. She even deprived me of the pleasure of telling a story. Sacre bleu.

After about fifteen minutes, we rose above the dense tree line and the vista completely changed. We saw the major peaks of the Alpine chain, the Lyskamm, and peaking behind, the Monte Rosa massif and its Dufour point, the highest in this region. I named as many peaks as I knew for Robin, even making up some that I couldn't remember. She was impressed, and that was why I was doing it. That was why I was saying anything in the last day or so.

Looming above us now was the station of the chair lift where we were to de-lift. A sign told us to raise the horizontal bar and prepare to get the hell off. I watched as the couple before us slid off to the side effortlessly. I was determined to do the same. A mountain goat–type man with a weathered face and mustache pulled the chair from under our butts, and Robin skied smoothly off to the left while I skied effortlessly for about ten yards, picked up too much speed, lost control, ran over some woman in flashy red Rossignol skis and a white jumper, and fell against a pile of plowed snow. Robin skied over with a grin on her face.

"You OK?"

"Fine," I said, more embarrassed that anything else. This was definitely not going to improve my self-esteem. No siree. I dragged my heavy ass up off the ground, dusted myself off, and pretended like nothing had happened.

"OK, let's go." Her voice trailed off as she began her descent. "Holy shit, she can really ski," I said aloud. "No snow plow, three quarter turns, just smooth parallel skiing." I figured that I would ski only when she wasn't looking—that way she wouldn't know how clumsy and awkward I was. Nothing worse

than an unsexy skier. That's as bad as wearing a bad bathing
suit. The good thing about skiing was that you couldn't see
what was happening behind you because you had to concentrate
on the terrain in front. I figured that I would just do my version
of the game "Red Light, Green Light" on the slopes. As soon
as Robin stopped, so did I. And as soon as she started, so would
I. She would never see me. I was saved.

This went on for a while: me making acrobatic saves on one
leg with poles flying to keep from falling, she swooshing down,
bending her knees, sticking her cute butt out, making elegant
turns, coming to a stop at virtually the same time. The problem
was that she was beginning to cover more of the hill than I
was, until finally she gestured that she would wait and I should
follow. No, go ahead, I motioned and pointed to a ski lift off
to the right that we could take back up. She nodded, turned
her skis toward the valley, and descended. I figured I needed
to catch up to her, so I threw caution to the wind—so what's
new?—and barreled down the slope after her. My uncle used
to say, "Why make turns when you can go straight?" Straight
down the hill I went after my lady love. The last thing I saw
before taking a tremendous tumble on my left side was that she
had made a neat turn at the ski-lift line. Right at that moment
I either lost my balance or panicked because I was exceeding
my speed limit. I leaned over, thinking that was a good way
to stop, and went into a spin. Snow went up my nose and one
ski came loose. When I had finally stopped moving, I wanted
to cry, and I looked up at the clear blue sky in confusion. I got
up on my one ski and saw Robin going to retrieve the other,
which had barreled down the slope like a cruise missile parallel
to the water. Luckily, it didn't strike anyone and planted itself
in a snow bank near a tree.

"Are you OK? You have to be more careful. You were going

way too fast." Robin was either concerned or annoyed. I couldn't tell which.

"You are right." My knees were shaking.

"The snow is so beautiful. This is great, Jean. Thanks." She kissed my red right cheek, the one I had fallen on. She put the ski at my foot.

"Thanks for retrieving it, Robin."

"No problem. Let's take this lift up the hill," she pointed.

"OK." I would have preferred to sit by the chalet and drink tea and get a sun tan, like rich brats from Milan with expensive ski equipment, but I wanted Robin to be happy and agreed. Now, I must repeat that I have a definite phobia about those lifts that have the frisbee-like thing that you pull down between your legs. It never quite has the right tension, and if you are not careful, you can easily cross tips and end up stranded on some precarious slope, never able to come down some narrow corridor of snow, beet red with embarrassment.

We got in the lift line, and I again watched the technique of those in front of me. A young man punches a ticket, then grabs the pole, pulls the seat down toward you, and then you tuck it under your butt. Looked simple. Robin grabbed the pole and swiftly tucked it beneath her with a smile. It was my turn. At that point, the attendant went off to answer a phone call, and I was expected suddenly to do everything myself. I struggled up to the point of attack, grabbed the pole with all my might, began to drag it between my legs, until I panicked and couldn't get it under there and settled for just placing it between my shoulder and my arm—the way I had seen some ski instructors do it. Even though this wasn't particularly correct technique, it would still be very hip and look good. Proud of my ability to improvise, I began to swish slowly up the relatively flat slope, my skis gently gliding over the humps in the snow.

All proceeded smoothly until we reached the sharp ascent. I started to get all off balance as the damn machine began to tug violently on one side of my body. I squeezed down on that pole with my arm for dear life until my biceps and triceps began to burn with overuse. I can't let go now. This is too dangerous; I'll never get back down, I reminded myself over and over again, repeating just hold on, just hold on . . . just hold on. Then I tried a different method. Perhaps if I tried to focus on something completely different, like the Knicks, or Robin's love, or my mother's lasagna. No, this wasn't working, my arm was burning in pain. OK, hold on, hold on. And somehow I did. After another thirty seconds, the terrain began to level off again and I felt the tension lesson in my arm. The finish was in sight. I had made it. I think my entire body had gone into some kind of survival overdrive gear, the way it must were I caught in a fire, or hanging by my fingertips on a ledge above Broadway, or taking my Ph.D. exams. I had found strength, which I never really knew I possessed.

At the top, I let go of the pole and skied down to where Robin was waiting, adjusting her mirrored sunglasses. We were way above the tree line now, and bright light reflected every which way off the snow, unencumbered by trees or rocks.

"This is spectacular, Jean."

"Yep, nothing quite like it." I was furiously rubbing my arm.

"Everything OK?"

"Sure." No need to tell her what happened, I was just glad to be alive. "Go ahead, Robin, I'll follow right behind." Skiing would be a breeze after that harrowing experience on the lift. I watched my love weave gently down the slope and followed her like a beaten dog.

We repeated the same itinerary for the next three days: After a passionate night of love making, we woke up in the afternoon and had a bite to eat. Robin conversed with my father, and we went skiing. Our faces had begun to take on that muskrat look, and our lungs were thanking us for the clean air. Fred had lunch with us New Year's Eve Day, taking a break from Virginia.

"Isn't the skiing the best in the world?" Fred said at the table. He could not say a cruel word about Champoluc, even if the skiing was better in the adjacent valley under the shadow of the Matterhorn.

"Yes," Robin responded. "I'm enjoying it very much."

"You know, we are lucky this year," I added, "because there hasn't been any snow here the last couple of Christmas seasons, and it's not like in the United States, where they can make some with machines." I ate another bite of my mother's lasagna.

"It snowed last year, Jean." Fred had to defend Champoluc at any cost.

"Did it? I seem to remember Mamma saying that it hadn't." I turned to the authority.

"No, Fred, there was no snow at Christmas last year. The people were desperate."

"There was good skiing later on in the season then."

"Yes, yes." Mamma placated him.

"There was a rash of avalanches," he insisted. "One demolished my friend Davide's house. Swept it down the valley." He made an accompanying gesture.

Yes, I thought to myself. That was a terrible tragedy. I went into a lesbian introspective conversation for one. The two town lesbians, a teacher and a nurse, were killed in that avalanche while they were walking their dogs behind their house. I kept this information to myself at the dinner table because if I mentioned it, there might be a sense that I opened my mouth only when I wanted to talk about gay women.

"That same avalanche took down cousin Albina's house

and blocked up the valley for three days. They had to bring bulldozers from the Fiat factory in Turin to dig a tunnel through it," Fred informed us.

Much of the dinner table banter at my house was recycled information. Still, the family reacted with amazed looks. I think it was another way to avoid sharing anything meaningful, like, say, feelings. I noticed my stomach begin to expand. This was a sign that I was suffering from nerves complicated by gas. I get that at the dinner table very often. It's fairly painful, and sometimes I pop Rolaids to lessen the tension in there. My abdomen gets so big, sometimes it looks as if there's a fetus in there—only it's too far up my torso to really look like one. I pretended that it was to myself a lot because I thought it might be the closest I ever got to carrying a child. I began to undo the top buttons of my pants and untucked my shirt. No one would ever notice.

"How is Virginia?" I asked Fred.

"Giving some kids ski lessons this afternoon. We are going to meet later for Gino's party.

After being prodded gently by my father, Robin began to talk about her experience in architecture school. She explained which courses were requirements and which course she enjoyed the most. The family listened in complete awe. I think that Dad's father wanted him to be an architect, but Dad opted for graduate school in literary criticism. Maybe my mother wanted me to be a lawyer, but I opted for music school. We generally did what we wanted in my family. Fred wanted to be an artist. He had the talent and the drive. He would make it: I knew it.

Robin impressed my family with her talk, even though at some points I could see my mother roll her eyes. She was right on. Robin was beginning to annoy me too with all this self-righteous, slimy corporate junk. I poured myself another glass of wine. And looked at Mamma.

"And then my boss called me into his office and congratulated me on my design. It was the most thrilling day of my life. I truly love that man." Robin concluded.

Real lesbians would never say the words "that man." We tend to stay away from anything to do with "man" because of our general mistrust of patriarchal hegemonic institutions. I don't think I've ever said that in my life. I'd rather opt for that guy, even that fellow, but never that man. Those words have far too much weight. I got up and began to clear the dishes from the table. I took my napkin, and as I'd seen my mother do countless times before, wiped the leftovers off of each plate into the garbage can. Then I grabbed all the glasses between my fingers, the knives and forks, and the pots on the stove. I placed them all in a blue bucket, walked over to the wood stove, and with two dishtowels, picked up the pot of boiling water that was perched on the black metal, poured the boiling water into the bucket, added some cold water from the faucet and some Italian dish soap, and began to wash the first dish. In the adjacent sink, I let the cold water run to rinse the dish and placed the rinsed dish in an overhead cabinet that had no bottom so as to allow each dish to drip dry into the sink below. A genial Italian idea, it saves counter space and relieves you from the drudgery of drying. Only one problem: as you extend your arm to place the dish into the overhead bin, the water from the dish drips down your sleeve. I guess you can't have everything.

"I haven't seen Jean do the dishes in years." Dad teased me. I wasn't in the mood.

"I haven't seen you do them since I was of the age to notice." I retorted. He was not amused.

"In fact, Jean, you tend to do very little around the house. You never help your mother," he continued.

"Well, what does Fred do? What do you do? Nobody helps Mamma," I responded. He was embarrasing me in front of Robin, and I didn't appreciate it.

"Still, I think that you do next to nothing."

"Screw you." I lost it. Robin was horrified.

"You shouldn't talk to your father like that." She added her two cents.

"This is none of your business, Robin." I stood my ground and tears began to form for the thousandth time in my eyes this month. I could never stand up to my father. He was too much of a bully. This is when my mother saved me, as usual.

"Walter, yoo are really a good-for-a-nothing. You can only talka, talka talka. You are a phony." My mother was on the attack. A good defense is a good offense, her motto. Then the two of them really started to go at it. Dad yelled you !?!?!, and Mamma said something back to him in Italian. I dropped the dishes and slipped into the living room. What a disaster. Fred came in to smoke a cigarette. Robin followed close behind.

"Sorry about all this. I don't know why he had to start with me," I began.

"Why did you get so mad at him? I think he was just kidding." Robin prodded.

"I'm not in the mood for his brand of humor. I think that he always wants to have complete control of the situation. Pisses me off."

"Calm down, Jean. I'm sure you are reading too much into it." Robin reasoned.

People with no self-control hate it when someone tells them to calm down. It generally has the opposite effect.

"Just lay off, Robin. Go think about Phil, or something." Ouch. The truth behind my anxiety had finally erupted. Robin let it fly by her. She didn't want to deal with our reality either. I grabbed her hand as if to apologize and led her upstairs. I needed to be close to her now and we made love to my parents' screaming. How bizarre. I was a tiger and flipped Robin on the sheets, and after five minutes she moaned with satisfaction. I rolled off of her in a sweat, not able to climax. Frustration set in; she was never attuned to my needs. I just usually came on my own, in a kind of masturbatory way, by rubbing myself on her leg or imagining sexy encounters with men and Robin.

I held her in my arms and rubbed the back of her neck. She rubbed my shoulder. We listened to the fighting downstairs finally subside and a door slam. My father had left—that was his usual routine. I lifted Robin's face up to mine and we kissed. I rubbed the inside of her thigh gently and dragged my fingers slowly into her wetness.

"Fuck me." She whispered into my ear. "Please."

And I did. And I turned her on her stomach and climbed on her back and thrust my fingers inside of her and slid my wet body over her ass until we came together. We fell asleep until it was time to celebrate the New Year. That was around five o'clock.

Chapter 12

A rap on the door woke us up. It was my mother.

"It's six o'clock; don't you have to get ready to go to Andrea's house for supper?"

"Thanks, Mamma," I said, half asleep. "We'll be right down." I can't imagine what she was thinking on the other side of that door. Her daughter was having sex with a strange woman in her house. One day she even walked into Martha and me having sex. Martha was on top of me. I heard the door open, and a gasp, and the door slammed shut.

"What was that?" Martha asked in horror.

"My mother. Keep on doing what you were doing. It felt good." And we started up again.

Robin jumped out of bed, put on a robe, and said she was going to take a shower. I said do whatever you want. My room smelled of woman's lovemaking, and I opened the window to let some cold fresh air in—briefly. I then went back to bed, rolled onto my stomach, and began to masturbate because I still didn't feel satisfied. I was so tense. My usual method was to place my third and index fingers firmly on my clitoris. Then I would press down on the palm of my hand. But most of the stimulation to orgasm came from my imagination or a Penthouse magazine I might have lying around the house. Sometimes I fantasized that I had a huge erection and was plunging it into a woman with huge breasts. Sometimes I fantasized that I was being attacked by four butch lesbians with large penises in the stall of the women's room. I tried to recall some of my favorite porno scenes from Channel J. I thought of all of these things together until I found the thing that worked. This time I imagined Robin being fucked by two men, one from behind and one from in front. I came in three minutes. Robin knocked on the door and let herself in. I jumped out of bed, grabbed my robe, and descended the stairs to the shower just in the nick of time.

The water in the shower was lukewarm, and I was done in forty-five seconds. I dried myself off with the red towel from Caldor and loped back upstairs. Robin was putting on a sexy black bra, the one I liked. I walked up behind her and rubbed the soft skin of her stomach.

"Don't get yourself all worked up again. I'm all clean," she warned me, as if I were really in the mood again. Please.

"No reason to worry," I assured her.

"Do you like this red sweater with the jeans?" she asked me, as if I were her husband.

"Yes, dear," I kidded her.

"I'm being serious. Does it look all right?"

"I said yes, and I mean yes." I had no patience for this kind of thing. She always looked good to me. She knew that.

"I want to look nice for your friends," Robin insisted.

"It's not that big a deal." I was in a foul mood.

"What's the matter with you, Jean?" Robin finally asked.

"My parents bother me. It seems that no matter what I do, they still have something to criticize. That whole dishes thing was unnecessary."

"He was just kidding," Robin assured me. "My father can be a jerk. But generally he is a pretty good guy. Maybe it has something to do with why you are gay?" She was veering off the subject.

"I really don't think so. As far back as I can remember, before I ever knew what a gay person was, I was gay. I didn't make a conscious decision about it. I just began to have feelings for girls in junior high and followed them around the school," I explained.

"I never felt that way for girls growing up." She was trying to talk herself out of being gay again.

"Some people don't realize that they are gay until much later in life. That doesn't mean anything. I am not any more gay than you because I felt it sooner."

"Who said I was gay? Why do you all find it so necessary to label me?"

"I'm not trying to label you, Robin. But it seems to me that you are having sex with a woman at this point and that probably makes you a lesbian. Wouldn't you say?" I was trying to convince myself of this, but I wasn't sure either about Robin's sexuality.

"I think that I am bisexual. That's how I wish to think of myself," she said resolutely.

"Suit yourself." This was hopeless. "I don't think it's about which sex you sleep with. It's about who you love and your ability to love at full capacity. By that I mean that if you truly loved me, you wouldn't give a shit about whether you were gay or straight—you would only care about me, about how we could be happy. You're just using that bisexual issue because you are afraid of admitting your feelings for me."

"I think that you are overestimating our relationship. I can't be committed to you. I can't be committed to anybody right now. I am too confused."

My heart was shattering. "How can you be so passionate in bed then?"

"It's fun."

The conversation stopped abruptly, and I finished getting dressed. Like my parents, Robin and I were very distant from each other, and like my parents, we didn't know what to do about it.

We walked downstairs, put on our coats and hats, and opened the door into the chilled air. It was already dark by six o'clock, and the stars hung over us so close that you could reach for them. Robin held my gloved hand in hers. I felt like I had to end. We decided to stop by the cafe to have a drink before the party. I said hello to the bartender, a mountain guide who had accompanied me on a trek to Switzerland and back when I was sixteen. He never remembered my name and sometimes called me Paola. I don't know where he got that from, but for some reason, I never corrected him.

We sat at a table furthest from the front door. The daughter of the mountain guide, I think her name was Anna, said hello. She was absolutely stunning: tall, bright blue eyes, translucent skin. If I lived in this town full-time, I would spend my life trying to become her wife. She had such a nice way about her too. Robin thought she was beautiful and said so after Anna had taken our order—two champagne cocktails, Italian style.

A tape of Bob Marley's greatest hits droned in the background. Italians love reggae. I don't know why. Snow began to fall outside. It gently rested on the ground, undisturbed by the wind, pedestrians, or cars. This was our last night together, and we toasted some bullshit toast to good times ahead and a prosperous New Year. Robin had to catch her flight back to New York reality in the morning. The thought of her leaving made me feel like dying. We talked about the Knicks and one of her deadlines and my piano teacher and some other things. I needed to throw up. I paid the bill at the counter, and we continued our march to oblivion.

My friends Marco and Mirella were married last year after being together for eleven years. I essentially grew up with them, and we spent summers climbing mountains, building forts, and throwing mud balls at the priest's house. We were caught once and had to spend an afternoon in the sheriff's office explaining why we had done it. Those were blissful days, before the pain of crushes and affection and sex messed me up. I was a very happy ten-year-old.

Because Mirella worked in a furnishings store, her apartment was the epitome of functionality and style: each knickknack made sense, each pillow matched. The couch was comfortable, and the dinner table was big enough for twelve. The kitchen was small but had all the necessary appliances: a dishwasher, juicer, toaster, and electric can opener. And believe me, the stuff did not look like it came from Caldor. Each gizmo was conceived of by some designer—you could tell. Everything was incredibly clean too. That's the thing about Italians, they tend to keep their homes clean and their bodies fairly dirty. Mamma always told me that Americans were just the opposite. They took twelve showers a day and kept a dirty home. Based on my experiences in both Italy and America, I had to admit that I had found my mother to be right.

I introduced Robin to the hosts and explained that she did not know any Italian, except for the usual silly spaghetti and cappuccino. When I said this, people laughed. Maybe they were just being polite? You know Italians are more polite than Americans, right? I think my mother and I have debated this point many times.

There were ten people at the party: Rossana and her husband Bruno, Marcella and her boyfriend Antonello, Silvana and her fiancè Stefano, the host and hostess, and me and my lesbian date. They thought we were some kind of American best friends, like Laverne and Shirley, or Lucy and Ethel. We probably could have hugged and held hands and kissed in their presence, and they would have chalked it up to some American thing.

Robin said yes to a glass of white wine and sat on the couch. She struck up a conversation with Marcello in his high school English. I wandered over to Marco and asked him how things were going. He said that his father's car dealership was thriving, he was learning a lot there, and he had just brought a new Lancia Delta, turbo, white, with red spoilers. I asked him if I could take it for a spin sometime, and he said no because he knew that I had cracked-up the family car a couple of years back. He knew me very well. I wouldn't lend me the car either. He told me that Mirella was doing well. She was working long hours in her parents' store, and they were planning to have a baby soon. My friends were definitely adults; I was still dating straight woman. What the hell was I doing? I wish I could have explained my predicament to Marco. He would have certainly understood. I was still safely in the Italian closet. I think my uncle Davide would beat the living shit out of me if he knew the truth.

I asked Andrea for another glass of red wine and sat down snugly next to my love. She was gazing into Antonello's eyes by now. It made me sick. Real lesbians would never look at a man so adoringly. There would definitely be some hint of disdain, some annoyed or bored look. I cut in.

"So how is school, Antonello? You are in business school, right?"

"Yes. I study very hard, but do not do so good. I, how do you say, fail two exams."

"That's too bad." Because he was talking to Robin, I suddenly felt angry at him—in a way I had never felt before. Good, I thought. He failed. One fewer Milanese businessman wouldn't be the worst thing for this world.

Robin still smiled at him and his cheesy Italian accent. I got up to talk to Mirella.

"I hear you and Marco want to start a family."

"Yes," she responded, after pouring me another glass of white wine.

"We feel ready now. Now that Marco and I have steady incomes. My mother is pushing me to."

"Those mothers. My mother would be happy if I went out on a date."

"You have so much studying to do. No time."

"Right, right."

"Your mother told me the other day that you weren't married yet because American women don't get married young because they have to worry about a career."

"She said that?" I was proud of her.

"Yes. It sounds like getting a Ph.D. takes a lot of time."

"I just passed my doctoral exams and have to start writing my dissertation."

"What are you going to write about?"

"I don't know. I thought something about Lucca in the fourteenth century. But I don't really know. I'm going down to Florence with my parents tomorrow to stay for a week. Maybe I'll think of something." I took a large gulp of wine.

"You'll do it. You always have." Though I only saw Mirella once a year, she knew me well.

"Can I help you with anything?" I asked politely.

"Yes, why don't you tell everybody dinner is ready. I'll get out the antipasti."

"Sure."

I stumbled into the other room, pried Robin away from Antonello, and informed the guests that it was time to *mangiare*. Cute, huh? Robin and I gingerly walked to the dinner table and sat down in the middle, next to each other. Marco took one end, and Mirella took the end closest to the kitchen so she could run in and out easily. Italians had no qualms about sitting at head of the table. In America we think it's bad form for some reason.

Marco poured everyone a fresh glass of white wine, and we made a toast to the New Year. "Salute, salute," rang through the room as we clinked our glasses together.

I pinched Robin under the table, and she gave me a big smile. We were in love. She wrapped her leg around mine, and we listened to the sound of Italian. Mirella brought out the first round of antipasti—prosciutto and melon. The orange slices gleamed under the light as they were passed around. I took four slices of melon and three of prosciutto, two more than anyone else at the table—but I didn't care. Robin asked me what it was. I said cured ham. And she said that she would try it. And I said do whatever you want. I think I was feeling pretty drunk by that time.

"You don't get this in New York," Mirella said to Robin in charming broken English.

"I think you can. I've just never tried it," Robin responded. She could have lied to make them happy. But she had to say something to show that she knew it all better."It's not as good in America, but we have it," I added.

We began to talk politics, about tensions in the Middle East and the crime rate in Manhattan. Robin contributed her two cents as I listened. And then Antonello said something really insane while we were talking about the economy.

"You know the Jews own everything in America, all the banks and the monies."

What? I thought to myself.

Luckily, Robin didn't really understand what he had just said. I was only a half-breed. But it enraged me twice as much.

"That is simply untrue," I spoke out, in an Italian that was suffering at this point from too much wine. "Jews don't own any more of America than Italians or any other minority."

"You are mistaken. Just look at the names of corporate executives, especially in the banks. Most of them are Jews."

"This is a ridiculous remark, Antonello. You should be ashamed of yourself."

He responded with "Learn your history."

I felt like taking the melon strip and sticking it up his nose, and slapping a piece of prosciutto on his forehead. I didn't. I let it slide. I had more pressing problems: Robin and my dissertation. Who cares about some misguided Italian? There were other battles to fight.

Mirella then brought out a heaping bowl of green and white linguine with pesto sauce. I could just die. My favorite. I loved any type of pasta, especially with pesto sauce.

Mirella carefully doled out each serving and then asked us if we wanted some fresh Parmesan. Robin smiled and stroked the inside of my thigh. I think I was starting to get a little out of control. And she whispered in my ear that I should stop drinking.

"Come on, Robin. It's New Year's Eve. You are supposed to get blitzed."

"I'm asking you not to," she repeated. Well, this only got me more frustrated because I had asked her nicely to stop seeing Phil and she didn't listen. Nope.

"I'll take your request under consideration," I slurred.

"Thanks," she said with that stupid smile she used to piss me off.

The pasta helped to soak up the alcohol in my system, so I drank some more to keep up that desired level of numbness. While Robin was talking to Mirella, I swallowed a shot of wine. No one was particularly talking to me, and I began to fall into a semi-comatose state of alcohol-induced bliss. I felt that my neck could no longer support the weight of my head. I let my chin rest on my chest for just a minute. Marco poked my side.

"Is everything OK?"

"Fine. I'm just feeling a little sleepy."

"I think it's the wine."

"No, no. I can handle it. You don't know how much I used to drink in college. Made me a pro."

Mirella brought out the main course of veal scaloppini. My favorite. "This is absolutely my favorite," I told her as she put the food on my plate—as if I were a baby.

We ate the veal and the desert, told some jokes, stayed away from the Jewish issue, and talked about architecture school. Marco cracked open a bottle of Digestivo Antonetto that he had left to cool on the balcony. We told some more stories and waited for the countdown to the New Year, even though it wouldn't be the New Year in New York yet.

"One minute to go." Marco checked his watch. Thank God—no stupid Time's Square ball. Just friends, the icy Alps, a pseudo-girlfriend, some champagne. At exactly midnight, the quiet of the Alpine town was ruptured by a barrage of firecrackers. It seemed that every kid and father in the town had set off some kind of colorful rocket from the roof of their house. You couldn't do that in New York. Marco and the other men cracked open the bottles of champagne and poured us each a glass. The couples kissed as Robin and I pretended that we were just pals. Excruciating. I touched her leg gently. This was our kiss.

"I love you, Robin." I whispered in her ear.

"Me too." She looked up.

"I can't wait to hold you. I want to make love to you."

"You are piss drunk. I asked you stop an hour ago." She

became very serious.

"I wanted you to stop doing a lot of things in the last month. You never listen to me. This is your punishment."

"You can be such a jerk sometimes." She looked out the window.

Marco filled Robin's glass, and I motioned not to fill mine. I had had enough an hour ago. I began to feel the room spin and limped off to the bathroom.

I looked into the Italian bathroom mirror in disgust. Who the hell was this shell of a person? I had been reduced to a drunken imbecile. I peed with all my might into the toilet, flushed, and washed my face to rinse off the alcohol that had permeated my skin. I made myself sick. Something had to be done about this situation.

I returned to the living room, thanked Mirella and Marco, said good-bye to the other couples, told them they should come to New York sometime, got Robin her coat, and led her to the door.

"Ciao," Robin said.

"Ciao," I said.

The cold air felt like a slap in the face. I began to walk with more assurance.

Robin wasted no time. "You were a real jerk in there."

"I can't help it. I feel like I'm going to die."

"What are you talking about?"

"You can't leave Phil, Robin. Don't you understand that it's killing me."

"Now we are back to that again."

"I want to be your one and only lover. I can't share you with anyone else."

"I can't do that, Jean. I can't make that kind of decision." Robin responded coldly.

"You are heartless." I grabbed her jacket and dragged her off the road into the snowy field. The snow reached our thighs and filled our shoes. I plowed a path for her and held her hand. The farther we progressed, the deeper we sank in the snow.

"Stop, Jean. I'm really getting cold."

I didn't. I kept plunging forward. Farther and farther from the streetlight we struggled, into the depths of the Alpine snow.

"Please, don't go any further." I let go of her hand and continued on. The snow numbed the pain in my heart.

"Please, Jean, come back. You are going to get sick. This isn't funny anymore."

I felt the snow grab on to my left shoe. It slipped off, and I continued walking in my socks. I marched for another ten paces and collapsed. I could see the stars laughing at me and the moon stick its tongue out. Robin made her way to me and shook me.

"Get up, you idiot. Get up. We are both going to be sick."

"Why can't you love only me, Robin? Why?"

"Just get up. You are going to die out here." She sounded panicked.

I got up on to my knees, the snow caked in my hair. And I said what I had been meaning to say for months.

"It's over, Robin. I don't want to see you anymore."

"Just get up." She avoided me.

"Pretend like I never existed, because after tomorrow, you will never see me again."

And after saying that, I felt the weight of the snow and the ice and the alcohol lift off my chest. It was over. This excruciating ride was over. We walked back to the house. I never did find that shoe.

That night I fell asleep on the living-room couch. Robin slept upstairs, and the next morning, very early, at some ungodly hour, my mother came down to make her usual cup of caffeine. Finding me prone on the couch, reeking of champagne and garlic from the pesto sauce, she gently shook my shoulder.

"Huh, what time is it?" I asked in a daze.

"Sixty-thirty," my mother said after checking her watch.

"I need to wake Robin up and take her to the airport." I jumped up from the couch.

"Piano, piano." My mother calmed me. "What happened last night? Why are you on the couch?" She seemed almost relieved that we were fighting.

"I can't tell you now. I was drinking too much. She got angry. I said things I shouldn't have. I need to talk to her."

I put on a sweater and dashed up the cold stairs to our bedroom. Robin was already awake, having risen at the sound of her alarm. There was no way she was going to miss that flight back to New York.

"Get dressed. We have to leave in ten minutes." She was hard as rock. I was a soft, amorphous mess, having transferred all my strength to her.

We had our usual breakfast of croissants, which my mother had thoughtfully laid out for us. Dad was still asleep, but Mamma tried to lighten the air by telling some stories. Robin and I did not speak much. Just looked at Mamma as she rambled.

I picked up her luggage, went to the garage, and started up the white Fiat Uno. A tin can on wheels, the model had single-handedly saved Fiat from sure extinction in the European car market. Bright white smoke came out the back. I jumped out and into the warmth of our kitchen. Mamma politely wished Robin a safe trip, even though I could tell she disliked her, and told me to drive carefully. She said that we would be driving to Florence at around one o'clock, so I shouldn't dillydally at the airport. I assured her that I wouldn't.

Robin hugged Mamma and thanked her for the hospitality. We were off, back down the mountain. Leaving Champoluc was always so difficult. Every summer, as the days got shorter, my parents took us away from this paradise and brought us back to Queens. It's a wonder I did not kill myself then.

Robin and I did not speak for the entire two-hour drive. We stopped at a rest stop, got a coffee, read the *Herald Tribune*, drove through the treacherous fog on the Turin-Milan highway, and made our way to the airport at Malpensa. I dropped her off at the departure area and went to park the car. I missed her already. I missed her to the point of wanting to drive the car into a ditch off the mountain road. I adored every inch of her.

I walked into the gate area to find her in line to check in her bags. She was only an hour early for the flight, and a long line had developed, rather Italian style, around the marble corridor. She looked frustrated.

"Just watch for the next open check-in person. It works like a charm."

Sure enough, a short Italian woman with long black hair made her way slowly to the empty station. We watched her every move until that decisive moment when she announced that her station was open. We were the first ones in line. After getting rid of her luggage, Robin said that I'd better leave, my mother was waiting for me back home. I agreed and hugged her, stroked the back of her head, gazed into her eyes for one last time; I told her that I would never feel like this for anyone else in my entire life, told her that I adored her. She nodded, grabbed my arm, stroked my hand, and disappeared into the crowd. I stood there watching, until her scent had dissipated with the sensation of her touch. The love of my entirely meaningless life had left me.

Chapter 13

By the time I reached the Alpine enclave of Champoluc, I had no more fluids left in my body because I had cried every last drop. The Fiat Uno and the shell of a person limped back home to Mamma and Daddy. Mamma was waiting on the porch, checking her watch.

"Goa finish packing yoo stuff, we leave ina ten minutes."

I dragged my hung-over rear out of the car and into my room, where Robin and I had made love for a week and where her smell still clung to the pillows and the sheets. I grabbed the T-shirt she had slept in that night and held it over my nose. Then I plucked one of her wavy brown hairs from the pillow and put it in my pocket. I could hear my mother yelling from downstairs to hurry up.

"I'm coming, I'm coming." I shoved all my belongings into the duffel bag: toothpaste and brush and extra tampons and socks and pornographic magazines and sweaters. I was ready.

Dad had the car running and packed. Mamma stood by checking her watch. I climbed into the back seat and put my duffel bag under my feet. I would use it later as a pillow. Dad said something clever about leaving the mountains behind, Mamma said this was the most special place on earth and why don't I come next summer, bring another friend, and I wished I was dead. For some insane reason, sweat was condensing on my forehead. I wiped it off with the sleeve of my flannel shirt. Dad put the car in reverse and we moved out. It wasn't long before I fell asleep. In fact, I slept for four hours. It was warm by the time I got out of the car at some supermarket in

Tuscany.

Dad said that he just wanted to pick up a few things for the house. Mamma said that we needed some bread and cheese and some more toilet paper. I said that I would rather just sit in the car, but they insisted I get out. So the D'Entreves family found a shopping cart in the enormous Italian parking lot and made its way into the Iper-Coop, the largest food store I had ever seen. It was like the Sears of Zabar's.

My legs were still numb over Robin. I was still in shock as my mother directed me to the dairy aisle and Dad peeled off to the salami area. I was going cold turkey.

"Wanta some yogurt?" she asked me.

"Whatever," I said despondently.

"Plaina or with fruit?" she asked.

"Whatever."

"I'll getta apricot, OK?"

"Fine," I said sharply pushing the cart toward the shelves that held the yogurt. She barely noticed that I wasn't talking.

"How about a milk? You want some a milk?"

"I'm too old to drink milk."

"I know, we need some butter. Go getta some over there." My mother was in bliss when she went shopping with me. I was convinced that she entered some kind of surreal world in department stores. Her heartbeat quickened, her eyes got bigger; there was a reason to live. It was like she just injected a shot of heroin into her veins. And I was part of her trip. When we drove to White Plains from the city, we first stopped at Loehmann's on Central Avenue, then Symm's, and finally Caldor in Yonkers. By the time we got to Caldor, I was exhausted and she was coming down from her high, so we stopped at Burger King for a Whopper before going in. Having recharged our batteries with junk food, Mamma led me into the maze of gizmos in

Caldor and picked out her final purchases of the day: a plunger for the toilet, another set of kitchen utensils for Italy, and a new bath mat for the red bathroom. I carried the packages to the car. My mission for the day was accomplished.

"How abouta some ricotta, Jean?"

"Whatever." I responded in my standard way.

"Mozzarella?" she said in the correct Italian accent. There were about fifty types to choose from.

"I don't really care what you get. I'm not hungry." Lack of hunger was one of the few things that got her attention.

"You aren't feeling a well. You have a stomach ache?"

"No, I just don't feel like eating."

"Whata is it?" she finally asked.

"It's Robin."

"I don't like that girla at all." She finally admitted. "She is so colda and arrogant."

"Come on Mamma, you barely know her."

"I canna tell. No," she paused. "I didn't like her a at all. Don't tell me you are going to ruina the rest of yoo vacation over her? Please spare a me, Jean."

"It's always about you, isn't it. I feel like I want to die, and all you think about is how it will affect you."

She reached down and put a piece of cheese into the bin. Keep shopping, she must have been thinking. Just keep shopping and this confrontation will simply pass.

"I need to tell you something, Mamma." She stopped dead in her tracks. "In fact we better stop and get some yogurt." I backtracked.

"Oh, my a God, whata is it?"

"I was pretty sick before I came over to Italy."

"What is it?" I heard a bit of terror in her voice.

"Herpes, I contracted genital herpes. I was sick as a dog for two weeks."

"Oh, my a God." She was paralyzed.

"There is no cure for it. You have to change your lifestyle. Stop drinking alcohol and staying out at night and eating junk food. I have also had all these yeast infections. They drive me crazy. Let's get some yogurt."

Now it was my mother's turn not to move. "You have a to tell your father," she insisted.

"I can't. You tell him. Anyway, it's none of his business."

"I always knew a this would happen. It's a sick."

I knew what she was getting at. "I didn't get the disease because I am gay, for Christ's sake. I got it because I was with a woman who sleeps with men."

"Thata terrible girla. Thata beeetch," she muttered.

"Please don't speak about her like that. I can't bear to listen to it."

An Italian lady motioned my mother to move slightly so that she could reach the gorgonzola. Mamma moved one inch to the left and said, "OK, Jean, tell me what yoo need to eat. I'll getta it for you. You have to a learn to eat right."

I drifted back into a semi-comatose state, leaning on the cart with my elbows.

We rolled into the produce section, and Mamma piled broccoli, zucchini, grapefruits, tomatoes, and celery into the cart. I can't possibly eat all that in a week. In fact, I didn't feel like eating anything for a while. But I nodded with respect each time she shoved something in. Dad caught up to us next to the fennel.

"Jean's gotta terrible news," my mother started. "She is a sick."

Dad got visibly nervous.

"Tella him, Jean, tella your father what you have."

"Mamma, this is very private stuff. I can't just tell him

here."

Then she told him herself. He looked shocked, but in his usual manner, tried to brush it off.

"Did you see a doctor?" he asked.

"Of course she a did. It's incurable. Canna you believe it? That little beetch. If I would have knowna, I would have made her sleepa in the snow by the garage."

"I'm not sure she gave it to me. The doctor says that I shouldn't blame anyone. I should have been more careful. That's all. I have learned my lesson now."

My family was visibly shaken. Not only had their lesbian daughter embarrassed them with her choice of sexuality, now they had to deal with the stigma of a venereal disease. I helped pile the groceries in the trunk of the car and slid into the back seat. Tuscany enveloped me and I was asleep again.

The house in Fucecchio sat on a small hill overlooking the town. The previous owners, who were German intellectuals, lived in it during the summer and winter breaks. They had entirely revamped the inside, putting up walls in the bottom floor to create a small separate apartment for their widowed mother. Each bathroom had been redesigned for utmost comfort, with showers and bidets. They even imported their own toilets from Germany, you know the ones with flat porcelain bottoms so that you can inspect what you made before flushing. It was also the only house in the region that had screens on the windows to keep the bugs out. Otherwise sophisticated Florentines spent most summer nights swatting enormous flies or inhaling Italian pesticides. The halls were covered with red Tuscan clay tiles, which glimmered when the lights were switched on. The kitchen was fairly big, and Mamma could use the dishwasher if she desired. I liked the bedrooms upstairs the best. Each had high ceilings and dark chocolate beams that crisscrossed overhead. My room was especially wonderful, overlooking the valley into the famous land where Leonardo ate *gelati* and squirted people with his makeshift water pistol during his youth.

Dad pulled the car into the garage at the back of the house, and Mamma and I squeezed out. I grabbed as many grocery bags as I could and my bag (we were forever carrying bags in this family) and waited, like a dog, by the front door for my father to open it. The Germans had even replaced the wooden front door with glass so they could sit inside during cold days and look out onto their property. So practical. Dad told me to dump the packages and make myself at home. Hey, wait, this was my home. I dragged my sorry ass up the stairs into my room and shut the door. My mother had put fresh sheets on the bed, and I could smell the dried lilacs that she had shoved under the pillow. I took off my jacket and shoes and jumped onto the bed. My butt sunk into the soft mattress until my feet were almost at the same level as my head on the pillow. The first thing I always do when I enter a room that I haven't been to in a long time, or a new room at a friend's house that I've never been to, is stare at each corner very deliberately. Then I close my eyes and make several wishes: first that my family and friends enjoy good health and then that the person I love is happy.

Having completed this ritual in my parents' house, I found the remote to the television and flipped on the Italian tube. A dubbed rerun of *Eight Is Enough* was on Channel 5. I never liked this show in English, so I moved on. The Italian evening news was on the next channel. A frumpy woman in her forties read the news in a deadpan voice as photographs of assassinations and world strife popped up. None of this clever repartee between anchor and correspondent. Just the facts. I moved on.

Next, I found the Home Shopping Network. This was unlike any I had seen in New York. A woman was selling a slimming machine, the kind with a wide canvas belt that wraps around the body and shakes the fat off of you. She was placing it around her hips, around her thighs, and shifting it down to her ankles. The cameraman zoomed in on her various body parts. I started to feel myself getting aroused by all this frenetic giggling and slowly slipped by hand inside my pants. As she shook so did my hand and after about five minutes, she put the canvas belt under her buttocks. I had an orgasm, rolled over, and shut the damn thing off.

I didn't move from that room for three days. Just vegetated in front of the Home Shopping Network. Let my mother in to give me food that I didn't eat. Hoped Robin would call and tell me she had left Phil. I did not take a shower or walk outside. Every once in a while my mother knocked on the door, but I told her to go away because I did not want to talk. The sun rose, hung around for a while, and sank for three days with no meaning. Until the day Mamma said, "Jean, I justa spoken to Miriam. She wants to see a you tonight."

"She does?" I perked up for just a moment.

"She is ona her way."

"But I'm not ready," I hesitated.

"Getta dressed. She'll be here a in ten minutes."

"OK." Miriam was the only person on the face of this earth whom I respected at this moment. I crawled out of bed, walked over to the dresser, and put on a fresh pair of underwear. I put on a white turtleneck, some jeans, and a heavy sweater. Glancing obliquely at the mirror, I realized my hair was incredibly unwieldy and ugly and my eyes had sunk into the recesses of my skull. God, I looked like hell. I quickly passed the brush through my hair and raked the knots out. That's when I heard the sound of Miriam's car making its way up the road to our house. My heart was suddenly filled with hope and expectation. My dog must have felt the same thing when he heard our car rumble up the road after school. I looked out the window and saw the shaky headlights of her car. My savior was arriving.

I put on the final touches to my outfit, opened the door of my prison cell, and walked downstairs. My mother and father sat in the kitchen, delighted that I had finally decided to come out. (Well, not really come out, they were certainly not happy about that.)

"You happy Miriam is a here?" my mother asked. I did not respond as I went for the door.

"See you later," I said with my first smile in three days, except for an occasional grin while I was watching the Home Shopping Network.

Miriam drove up to the house in her black Volkswagen Golf GT. She opened the door of the passenger side and motioned me to come in. What I liked best is that she did not even get out to say hello to my parents. She was going to devote her energies solely to me tonight.

"Come in, Jean," she directed me. I bounded into the car.

"Oh Miriam, thank you so much for coming," I said sincerely.

"Your mother called and said you were despondent, that you didn't feel like getting out of bed."

"I don't feel like doing anything."

We drove down the road in silence. I looked at the twisted olive trees that covered the horizon like thorns on a rose bush. Miriam's house was up on a hill above my father's. She had bought it about five years ago. Hers was bigger. It was a bit more expensive, though she shared the huge old villa with three other tenants. Miriam drove at a fast pace, skimming the side of the narrow roads, causing pebbles to fly off behind her. I watched contentedly as she changed gears and finally pulled off to her apartment.

"This is it," she said in her fluent English with a German and Tuscan accent.

I opened the door and asked her if I needed to lock it, and she said no, this wasn't New York. She led me through the thick front door that led onto a typically cold Italian marble floor. The kitchen opened up on our right. I asked her if I could see the rest of the house, but she said no because we were here for business and did not want any distractions. She flipped on the kitchen light and told me to sit on the chair by the fireplace. The fire was still smoldering and giving off heat as I moved near it. Miriam asked me if I would like a cup of tea, and I said yes, thank you.

"This is a beautiful kitchen," I told her to break the ice.

"Isn't it?" The conversation stopped again. I watched her prepare our tea. After putting the two Italian porcelain cups on the table, she went into a back room and pulled out some fresh logs to put on the fire. They sizzled as the bark burned.

"OK. Now we can begin." Miriam handed me the tea and sat down. "Close your eyes and feel the heat of the fire in your soul. This is the strength you possess inside of you. You have lost it temporarily because of unhealthy relationships and self-neglect. We must work to repossess the strength." She put the tea down and began to move her hands above my body in a circular fashion. I could feel her energy penetrate my body and relieve some of the tension that I had stored up in my soul for so many months.

"Now, tell me what has been going on," Miriam said. I told her that I was madly in love with Robin, the architect who had a boyfriend. I told her that I had gotten herpes from her, and that I did not know what the hell to write about for my dissertation. And then I told her that I wanted to die.

"Go ahead, just kill yourself then," she said in a rather upbeat voice. She frightened me.

"What do you mean?" I asked.

"If you really feel like you should kill yourself, you should go ahead and do it. But I don't think that's what you really want. You are just searching for someone to save you. You must learn to save yourself." I still didn't understand what she meant.

"Jean, why do you think that you contracted herpes?" she asked me.

"We had very unsafe sex and she had a boyfriend. I was naive."

"But that doesn't mean that you had to get herpes. Why do you think that you got it?" she asked again.

"Because I am an imbecile."

"You still don't understand."

"Why do you think you got herpes as opposed to an ear infection, or a headache, or the flu?"

I looked at her in a blank way.

"You got it because you had lost track of yourself. The energy inside of you finally rebelled and signaled to you that you were abusing your body: you were abusing your body by having a love interest that was not reciprocating your caring. You got sick in the only place you could have, in the place where you make love. It's clear as day. Your body wanted you to stop doing it, so it created a sickness in that area.

"My friend was married to a man who had been abusing her. She finally moved out of the house with her child. This guy kept calling her, and she listened to his sad story every night. She did not ask him to stop or hang up the phone. She just listened until one night she got an excruciating pain in her ear. She went to the doctor, who told her to take all this medicine to relieve an infection, but the pain persisted. She called me one day to tell me that she had this pain in her ear that would not go away. I advised her to stop talking to her husband on the phone. The pain went away in one day.

"Do you understand what I am trying to tell you? You have been going from one relationship to another, without giving yourself a chance to figure out who you are, what your needs are, and what kind of person you want to be with. The herpes is a signal to spend time getting to know yourself, to stop having sex, and to move away from Robin."

"But I love her," I had to interject.

"She is not good for you. She is not good for anyone right now."

"I can't go on without her." My desperation reared its ugly head again.

"You must learn to. It is the best thing for you. You must learn to trust yourself, learn from yourself. You have the ability to do so. Let Robin go. She doesn't need you either now. She is using you like a crutch. She needs to learn to stand on her own." When Miriam spoke about how Robin needed to be rid of me, it somehow made me feel better. I was no longer responsible for Robin's happiness. Weird how that was. Nevertheless, I insisted that I could not be without her.

"Jean, you cannot make her into somebody she is not. You are not appreciating her in the right way. When I was a child," she began another parable, "I had terrible acne—blotches all over my face. I sat in the sun and kept my face as dry as possible because I thought that my acne was caused by grease. One day an old woman in the neighborhood saw me sunning myself on the porch and told me to stay out of the sun. She told me that instead of keeping my face dry, I should try putting some cream or moisturizer on it. At first I thought she was crazy, but then I put some of my mother's cream on my face. After three days, I saw a marked improvement. I had thought that my face should be dry, but instead I needed to keep it moist. Do you understand? You are seeing the world in one way now, when you should experience it in a completely opposite manner."

I was beginning to see her point.

"You need to be independent, not spend your time in a painful relationship," she concluded.

"But it's impossible for me to do that right now. I feel so empty."

"That's the point. You need to fill your life with other things besides these relationships. With things you like to do that are wholly yours. That don't involve other people," she insisted.

"I can't, I can't live without her." Then Miriam reached for my right hand. She took the ring that she wore on her hand and placed it into my palm. She closed my hand around it and told me to feel the energy of the white pearl throughout my body. I sat mesmerized, looking into her eyes. They were green with bright red sparkles, like those super rubber balls we played with as children. I felt myself relax for the first time in three months. Tears rolled down my cheeks as I allowed joy to enter my soul.

"Now, Jean, you must allow your spirit to prosper in your body. You must nurture yourself. Robin cannot be there with you on this new journey you are about to begin," Miriam reminded me.

"I think I understand." And I wasn't lying this time.

"Let us focus on your work. What are you going to write about in your dissertation?" she asked seriously.

"I had an idea about doing a project on the archives of Lucca.

I don't know. I'm not very inspired by the idea. I don't want to spend the next year of my life isolated in Italy, with no chance of meeting anybody in some dusty archive. I can't even motivate myself to think about it."

"Well," Miriam suggested, "perhaps you ought to work on something else. I don't feel that Lucca is the right topic for you. You must try something else."

"Like, what? I can't do women composers because I won't get hired in this conservative job market. Feminists are not in. I love the music and art of fourteenth-century Italy. They make me feel alive." I stopped.

"Perhaps you should do something with that," Miriam advised.

"But the topic is so vast. I don't know." I was whining like a typical graduate student. It was terribly unbecoming.

"A topic will come to you in the next three days. I am certain," Miriam assured me.

"I hope so. I think a great deal of my anxiety stems from the fact that I have no direction."

"I'm sure that's the case. Go visit some of the Tuscan towns in the vicinity, San Gimignano, Volterra, Siena. Let the culture and energy penetrate your soul. I think you should take an afternoon and sit in a monastery.

I thought she was way off base with this last suggestion, but I listened anyway. I felt warm inside. The fire was hot and Miriam's ring seemed to pulsate in my hand. I gave it back to her. Our session was over.

She drove me home through the humid Tuscan night. We did not say a word. The green lights of her dashboard reflected off of her veiny hands. Her graying curly hair spun wildly down her neck. She was tired. She had transferred her energy to me. She had begun the healing process, and now it was up to me.

We pulled up to the house. I kissed her good night. She held my hand one last time.

"Things will be better now," she said, looking me straight in the eye. I thanked her with all the love I had in my soul, got out of the car, and waved good-bye. I stood on the same spot for what seemed an eternity as I watched my savior in her Volkswagen Golf GT motor down the road, make a left turn at the intersection, and motor back up to her house. God, or whatever energy rules over us—I always had to qualify—God bless Miriam. I turned around and went back into the house.

I spent the next two days looking at frescoes that contained images of people playing music. First, I took the train into Florence to see the bagpipe and fiddle players frescoes by Andrea da Firenze in the Spanish Chapel in Santa Maria Novella, the fantastic church adjacent to the train station. I purchased ten postcards of each musical instrument and bought some souvenir slides for later use. The next day I took the local train to Siena and went to the Palazzo Pubblico to see a huge mural called the *Effects of Good Government in the City*. This picture has ten women dancing in a square. I bought a poster of the picture, slides, and more postcards. Then I took the train to Pisa to see the musicians in the fresco called the *Triumph of Death* by Buffalmacco. I loved those frescoes. I would write about the meaning of the musical figures in fourteenth-century Italian secular painting. My dissertation was slowly taking shape, and the cloud of uncertainty was lifting. Robin didn't call me that entire week. I would tell her it was over when I got home. I needed to work on my studies.

Miriam and I had one last chat the night before I left for the United States. She invited me out for pizza at the local pizzeria. I told her that I had found a topic and she said, "I know." She had spoken to me in a dream. I told her what the topic was and she said, "I know."

"You had the answers inside of you the entire time. You just were afraid to look."

"What should I do when I get back? What should I do about Robin?"

"Tell her that you need time to yourself, that you are working on your dissertation. Tell her you need to learn to be on your own."

"OK," I nodded.

"I think you ought to seek professional help," Miriam said in a firm tone.

"What do you mean?"

"I think you should see a therapist. It would help you immensely."

I could not believe she was telling me this.

"Why?"

"You were very depressed when I saw you last."

"Do you think I have a psychological problem? You are scaring me," I said.

"I went to the university for three years to study psychology. I wanted to study the mind but realized that their methods were too limited. Still, I know the benefits of therapy and I think you should go. Do it for your own sake. You will feel much better."

I listened to the earnestness in her voice and agreed with her suggestions. I would do whatever she said.

"You must learn to detach yourself from your parents. You are too enmeshed in their lives." She was raising her voice now. "You need to be on your own. Get out of their house. Live your own life."

I felt her energy. She was giving me one last push.

"And be open to new possibilities."

My healing was beginning. I thanked her again. We hugged and she dropped me off at home.

That evening I packed my bags for the trip back to New York. I watched the Home Shopping Network and masturbated. I thought about my new dissertation topic and wrote some ideas in my composition book. The first three chapters had already taken shape, and all I had to do was think of two more. I thought about what I would say to Robin when I talked to her again. I would tell her that I was going to refocus my energy on me. I flipped to the Playboy Channel and watched a bunny jump into an enlarged champagne glass and spin around in the water with her crotch facing me. I thought that was pretty fun and erotic. Then I watched a skit about a woman undressing in her bedroom while some guy peers through a peephole. The voyeur within a voyeur motif; I liked this, and it made me come. I fell asleep.

Chapter 14

NEW YORK CITY

My plane arrived at Kennedy Airport at three o'clock in the afternoon. I quickly found my bags on the carousel and marched them toward customs. Dad always warned me not to go to female customs agents because they are more thorough. The men tend to let you pass quickly. I thought I would challenge his thesis and paid the consequences. A blond-haired woman from Long Island, possibly a lesbian but it was hard to tell, made me open my Caldor's bag and, like those Russian wooden dolls that open up to smaller and smaller dolls, she made me open every medium to tiny package that I had in that damn bag. She even insisted that I open the little case that held my tampons. This was pissing me off. But you can't say anything to them. She probably thought I was carrying some drugs like my brother used to do. After seeing that her badge read Gina Di Pasquali, I made some small talk about Italy and how it's so beautiful. She did not smile or look up from bag-scavenging. Probably could sense the phoniness in my voice.

"OK, you can close it all up," she finally concluded.

I moved my junk to the side and began to zip everything up. It was the next fool's turn to be searched and humiliated. Dad was right in this case.

I lugged my stuff out to the taxi stand and waited for the next available cab. It was warm and muggy on this January day, and I was relieved that I had not walked into a piercing wind of a New York winter day. A large man asked me where I was going. I told him the Upper West Side, and he pointed me to a cab. I jumped into the back seat. It smelled of cheap air freshener, which was better than underarms, a favorite of many New York drivers. He sat on a mat of beads and listened to the top-40 station. His name was Jan, and he must have been about thirty-five years old, probably with a wife and two kids who lived in Queens. I sat back and enjoyed the ride while occasionally glancing at the meter. After we crossed the Triboro Bridge, I told him to take 125th Street to the West Side because it was the fastest route. He nodded, and I was happy to let him know that I knew New York and would not be taken for a ride.

We reached home. I paid the guy forty-five dollars. He pulled my bags out and I made for the door. The keys were easily accessible in my fanny pack, and I happily opened the door to the apartment building and my new life. I couldn't wait to talk to Robin. I had missed her intensely. She had never called me in Italy.

"Hey," I said with all the love I could muster in my voice. "I'm back."

"Hi, Jean." Then a pause. "I can't talk to you right now. I'm in the middle of a meeting. Can I ring you later?"

"Sure," I said as my heart sank. "Sure, speak to you later." I felt the same kind of anxiety I had experienced before leaving for Italy and talking to Miriam. This had to stop. I decided to call Rachel.

"Hey." She knew it was me.

"Hey, welcome back." Rachel was happy to hear my voice. "So how did it go?"

"OK. You mean with Robin?"

"Yeah, and how are your folks?"

"I'm going to break it off with Robin. We had a terrible fight."

"Jean, she is not right for you."

"I know, I know. I have realized it. I just needed some space from her. Rachel, what's the name of that shrink you used to talk to?"

"Deb Bernstein. She is the greatest. Do it, Jean, you'll love her."

"How did she help you?" I asked.

"She taught me to relax and have confidence in my own choices. She helped me understand my family and feel better. Here I'm going into clichés. Call her right away, Jean."

"I don't know if I'm ready for a shrink." I hesitated. "I'm not completely crazy."

"Do it, Jean," she insisted.

"My parents will think that I am out of control."

"That's why you have to go: to stop caring about what the hell your parents think. Do it, Jean. Hold on, let me get you her number."

I went over what Miriam had said in Italy.

"Here, Jean." Rachel read the numbers to me. "Call her, OK?"

"Want to meet for dinner later? I asked.

"OK. I'll see you at six-thirty. Bye."

I looked at the numbers she read to me for three minutes before picking up the phone to call Deb. Was I really crazy enough to need a shrink?

Dr. Deb had a pleasant voice on her answering machine. I told her that I had been referred to her by Rachel and that I wanted to start lessons, or sessions, or whatever they were called. I left her my number. Done—that was finished. I put my dirty laundry in the hamper and my toothbrush in the porcelain holder, checked if there was anything to drink in the fridge, and poured myself a glass of club soda. The phone rang. It must be Robin. My heart leapt with joy.

"Hi, I have missed you," I said to her.

"Me too. It's good to hear your voice."

"Can I see you tonight? We need to talk."

"No. It's really not possible. I'm working on some final edits to a proposal. My team is meeting tomorrow morning to look at it." I started to get frustrated.

"I need talk to you about our relationship. I think we need to take a break from each other."

". . . OK," she said quietly.

"I need to find out who I am. I'm going to see a shrink." I waxed confessional. I told her about what Miriam had said. She listened in silence. "You know that it will be excruciating for me not to see you. I am in love with you. But I think that it is the best thing for right now."

"I guess so." She did not put up any resistance.

"I will miss you incredibly." I felt my heart ache already.

"Me too." There was silence.

"Take care, Jean," she said.

"Take care, Robin."

And as innocently as it began, it was over. She had put up no resistance.

I had dinner with Rachel that night. She told me about having oral sex with her boyfriend, and I told her about the great sex I had had with Robin. I told her about my new dissertation proposal, and she told me about the paper she had just written. I loved her. We talked about the prospect of seeing Deb.

"Miriam told me to think of her when the going gets tough. She will send me energy through the wind. When I feel the wind upon my face, Rachel, it's a sign that Miriam is talking to me."

Rachel looked a little puzzled. "I'm happy you can find strength in her. You need to find out what your family is all about. What their motivations are, how you react to them."

"Hey, Rachel, did you ever consider becoming a shrink. I think you'd be great," I said enthusiastically.

"That's what Deb told me once. I don't know. I'd have to go to school for six more years," she said wistfully.

"Speaking of school, I've got to go to the library tonight. I want to start researching for my dissertation."

"But you just got home."

"I feel like the thesis is going to help me deal with Robin. I've got to refocus my energies. Plus I finally know what I want to write about."

I gave Rachel a rough sketch of the chapters. She seemed impressed and told me to go for it. We ate the last bite of our pizza, kissed each other on the cheek, and said our goodnights.

Epilogue

At home I gathered a yellow pad, some pens and pencils, and my pocket Italian dictionary, and put them in my knapsack. With a skip in my step, I put on my jacket, shut off the hall light, and took the elevator to the ground floor. College Walk glimmered with sparkling white Christmas lights. My step broke the slates of ice that had formed between the cobblestones. The journey to completing my dissertation and starting my life had begun.

Rereading these pages about my exam and lost love, I began to understand what really happened, about the emptiness inside that cannot be filled by other people. I hated what I was doing, but could not stop doing it. Robin disgusted and amazed me, just as I did myself. She was my mirror as well as my muse. I saw myself in her and tried to kill her as I ultimately tried to kill myself.

It took hitting rock bottom to reassess my life. Or, to paraphrase Dante, I had to see myself in the dark wood, with no way out. I had to deal with how unhappy and unfulfilled I felt before the whole mess began. With Martha I was unhappy; alone I was unhappy; with friends I disliked myself. I could not look at myself in the mirror.

My family and the woman I was dating at the time created my identity, like a novelist or a painter on a canvas. But I wasn't a particularly well-rounded character. I was a good person only in relation to how I was perceived. If I treated Martha kindly that day, I was worthy; if my Mamma yelled at me for not getting her Lotto tickets, I was a failure. If Robin had sex with me, I was decent; if she had to work that night, I was an embarrassment to myself.

I needed to do things for myself. I needed to brake the cycle of unhappiness. This takes time. I worked on my dissertation six hours a day. I read Buddhist texts, played basketball, and went dancing at night. And during all those moments when I had time to think empty thoughts, I thought only about Robin. The first few months I dreamt of her every night. I wished she would leave Phil and come back to me. I felt nauseous in the morning, and when my brother knocked on the door to see if everything was all right, I would sob, yes, just please leave me alone. But slowly these feelings subsided, and with the coming of each new moon, I could tell that I was improving. I had put my mind to it; I had to change.

In therapy I looked at my family and my relationships with friends and began to recognize the patterns and the mistakes. I went twice a week for three months, sobbing the entire forty-five minute period. Deb helped to unravel my life, and laid the strings flat on the table, and I began to see the truth about who I was, not how I was perceived by others. I have no idea what love is. Only what it meant to be obsessed and helpless. I had tried to find comfort in a violent sex life. Now I needed softness and caring and distance from my family. I loved and respected my parents, but I just did not know how to accept their mistakes. I knew that deep down inside, I was a nice, caring person. I wanted good for the people around me and for myself. I would make this my goal—from now on.

And what of Robin? I spoke to her on the phone a couple of times during the first months. She continued to work seventy-hour weeks. I think Phil did move in with her, eventually. Yes, I hear they live together now on the East Side.

You see, I cut off all communication with her, quit the rugby team, and sent back the few things she had given me. Miriam had opened the way to a new beginning, or maybe it was simply a matter of living or stagnating, and I chose change.

Table of Contents

European Press Fiction

Giampaolo Aiuti	*La Storia che Verrà*
Nora Beck	*Fiammetta* *(Trilogy)*
Valentina Fiorineschi	*L'Istante*
Maurizio Ricciardi	*L'Eredità*
Alison Castelli	*Visions of Italy*
Autori Vari	*Il Respiro dei Colori*

EPAP publications on:

http://www.e-p-a-p.com
http://www.europeanpress.eu